"You think Mary's killer could come after you?"

"If you think it's even a remote possibility, then I should leave now."

"No. You're not leaving."

She watched as his gaze drifted down to her mouth, then lower to the mounds of her breasts. In an instant, his eyes snapped away, but she had caught the look and her entire body responded to it in a flash.

No, she told herself. *No.* But it had happened, and she couldn't deny that it had. Standing there, looking at Dom as he turned back to his chair, she knew she was getting into deep trouble.

She had come here, hoping to find a clue to a killer—not a romance, not a passion, not a fling. Nothing was going to change that, not her unexpectedly strong response to him, or even the way her arm tingled where he had touched her.

She looked down into her coffee as she waited for her suddenly racing heart to slow down. Wrong time, wrong place, wrong guy.

★ ★ ★

P9-DHJ-965

Dear Reader,

It's often easy to forget that women are heroes, too, especially when we think of war.

This is the story of one such hero, and the family she left behind when she was killed. Her husband and her young sons face a future without her, left with only her heroism as comfort.

This is also a story about how justice can become an end, as well as a means, and how justice is not always the best answer. It certainly won't heal the wounds.

It's also a story of love, of how two people surmount their own internal obstacles to find a way to grow together.

In the end, it's all about love.

Enjoy!

Rachel

RACHEL LEE

The Final Mission

Harlequin

ROMANTIC
SUSPENSE

Recycling programs
for this product may
not exist in your area.

ISBN-13: 978-0-373-27725-4

THE FINAL MISSION

www.Harlequin.com

Printed in U.S.A.

Books by Rachel Lee

Romantic Suspense

An Officer and a Gentleman #370
Serious Risks #394
Defying Gravity #430
★*Exile's End* #449
★*Cherokee Thunder* #463
★*Miss Emmaline and the Archangel* #482
★*Ironheart* #494
★*Last Warriors* #535
★*Point of No Return* #566
★*A Question of Justice* #613
Nighthawk #781
★*Cowboy Comes Home* #865
★*Involuntary Daddy* #955
Holiday Heroes #1487
★★*A Soldier's Homecoming* #1519
★★*Protector of One* #1555
★★*The Unexpected Hero* #1567
★★*The Man from Nowhere* #1595
★★*Her Hero in Hiding* #1611
★★*A Soldier's Redemption* #1653
★★*No Ordinary Hero* #1643
★★*The Final Mission* #1655

Silhouette Shadows

Imminent Thunder #10
★*Thunder Mountain* #37

Silhouette Books

★*A Conard County Reckoning*
★*Conard County*
The Heart's Command
  "Dream Marine"

Montana Mavericks

Cowboy Cop #12

World's Most Eligible Bachelors

★*The Catch of Conard County*

★Conard County
★★Conard County: The Next Generation

RACHEL LEE

was hooked on writing by the age of twelve, and practiced her craft as she moved from place to place all over the United States. This *New York Times* bestselling author now resides in Florida and has the joy of writing full-time.

Her bestselling Conard County series (see www.conardcounty.com) has won the hearts of readers worldwide, and it's no wonder, given her own approach to life and love. As she says, "Life is the biggest romantic adventure of all—and if you're open and aware, the most marvelous things are just waiting to be discovered." Readers can email Rachel at RachelLee@ConardCounty.com.

For FarWestGirl, a dear friend who helped with all her horse experience to bring this story to life. The mistakes are mine, but I made a lot fewer of them because of you, dear FarWestGirl. This one is for you.

Chapter 1

Dominic Mason stood behind his house, staring out over expansive pastures. The night held an autumn nip that warned of coming frost even though it shouldn't happen for another month or so. Regardless, he was nearly ready for the change in seasons.

He'd already brought most of his horses in from summer pasture. Only a few still needed to be gathered up. The hay had been mown and moved into the drying sheds that would protect it from most of the winter snows and make it easy to feed his herd over the long approaching winter.

Next month he'd sell a lot of his stock to ranchers, rodeos and breeders. His announcement of his annual sale had drawn a larger than usual amount of interest. Apparently his reputation for quality was growing.

He could see the dark shapes of his horses scattered around, quiet in the moonlight, not moving much. There was still plenty of ground forage for them, as he'd mowed early enough to allow for some regrowth, but at the moment they seemed more intent on resting. Even the dogs were invisible right now, probably quietly lying among the herd they watched over.

Just as his two young sons slept in the house behind him. Seven-year-old twin boys, the light of his life, and his agony, too, since their mother had been killed.

Annoyed with the direction of his thoughts, he gave his head an angry shake, then reached up to resettle his battered Stetson.

Another winter coming. Another winter alone. At least the rest of the year he could keep himself busy enough for three men, keep so busy he couldn't do much thinking. But once the snow flew, life would narrow. The outdoor activities that kept him so busy, the kids being off school, all that would give way to intensive training in the enclosed, battered arena off behind the barn.

But not yet. A chilly autumn night was a far cry from the blows of winter. And he had the sale next month to get ready for, the horses to choose to show.

He thought he heard a car coming up his drive, but sounds were deceptive at night, especially this close to the mountains. He couldn't imagine a single reason why anyone would be coming out here so late. All the reasons for such a visit were safely indoors or already dead. Well, except for Mary's parents, and they were about as hale and hardy as any sixty-somethings he'd ever known.

He turned anyway, because the boys were sleeping in their beds and he didn't like them to be alone long. Not anymore. Not since the illusion of security had been stripped from him two years ago.

The dirt and gravel crunched beneath his feet. Moonlight reminded him he still needed to till the summer's garden, now mostly a mess of weeds and stalks of dead plants, their bounty gone for the year.

With Mary, he'd enjoyed the winters. More time for them to spend together, fewer other demands. He'd been like one happy bear, burrowing into his den, venturing out only to look after his stock, work on training or to make an occasional supply trip to town.

Those trips lingered brightly in his memory. They'd always made a good time of the shopping, treated themselves to a meal at the diner, sometimes even sprang for a movie. But the long winter nights also remained bright in his mind— nights of playing games, laughing, reading, loving, just being together.

Now only desolation remained, and two little boys that he loved more than life. Two little boys he couldn't see without experiencing a pang for all they had lost, for all he had lost.

"Boss?"

He looked around to see his foreman, Ted Walking Bear, coming his way from the bunkhouse behind the barn.

"Yeah?"

"A car just drove up."

"I thought I heard one. I'll take care of it. Probably somebody's lost. Good night."

Ted touched the brim of his cowboy hat and headed back for the bunkhouse.

Quickening his pace, thinking of his boys, Dom hurried around the outside of the two-story frame house, rather than entering through the back mud porch as usual.

Sure enough, as he rounded the corner, he saw a vehicle pulled up in front. One he didn't recognize. The brilliance of the moonlight had kept him from seeing the headlights as the car approached, he guessed. They were off now, though.

Unease pricked at him a bit, but he tamped it down, telling himself it arose only because one time when strangers had driven up to his door it had been to tell him his wife was gone.

Other strangers had come since, but not at night. To buy

horses. To sell him things. To try to convert him. To save his soul. The last always made him want to laugh. He figured any soul he had left had pretty much shriveled from grief and anger.

A sound drew his attention to the porch. He looked, and even though the roof cast deep shadows on the wide veranda, he could see a woman in a long, dark coat standing there.

"Can I help you?" he asked. Automatic courtesy.

"Mr. Mason?"

"Yes."

"I'm Courtney Tyson. I knew your wife."

He'd had other visits from Mary's friends from the National Guard. Even so, his heart slammed a bit. When those friends wanted to visit, they called first, gave him a warning of what was coming, even gave him an out if he just couldn't bear it.

This one had come without either courtesy. "A call would have been nice." He hated the unfriendly edge to his tone, but anger had stirred in him. Showing up like this without warning didn't seem either thoughtful or friendly.

"I'm sorry," she said. "Maybe I should explain. I'm from the Naval Criminal Investigative Service. No, Mary didn't do anything wrong. But I didn't want anyone to know I was coming."

"Why not?"

"Can we talk?"

Lead settled into his stomach, sickening him. He wanted to say no, to send her on her way, forbid her any chance to reopen the most painful chapter of his life. He'd mostly made peace with it, except for an occasional errant stir of anger or grief, and he wanted to keep it that way.

But curiosity had already set its hook, and he was a neighborly man by nature. You didn't send a friend of your wife's off into a dark, cold night without at least offering coffee, hearing her out. She'd come a long way, evidently, all because she wanted to talk to him.

He hesitated a moment longer, sensing his life was about to change inalterably once again, and that he wasn't going to like it much more this time.

"Come on in," he said, hoping he didn't sound grudging. "Just be quiet. The boys are sleeping."

"Kyle and Todd?"

So she knew their names. Maybe that made him feel a smidgeon better, maybe not. "Yeah."

He rounded the porch until he reached the steps, then led the way into his house. A woman's light step sounded alien now, and made him wince a bit, reminding him of the sound of Mary's high-heeled dress boots, the ones he'd teased her about, swearing she was going to break an ankle. She'd always retorted that they made her feel feminine, which she needed after time in cammies and desert boots, or after wearing Wellingtons to muck out a stall.

He would give damn near anything to tease her like that again.

In the kitchen, he waved Courtney Tyson to a seat at the round oak table that was covered in some oilcloth and started a pot of coffee.

"I'll be right back," he said. "I want to check on the boys."

"Sure."

Her voice was soft, quiet, maybe filled with as much dread as he was. The sound, while it was appealing at one level, made his scalp prickle. Something bad was coming. He knew it in his gut.

Upstairs he found the boys racked out. They were seldom quiet sleepers, so he had to tuck legs and arms back onto the mattresses of the bunk bed, adjust the covers against the chill of night.

And he noticed, as always, how sweet they smelled after their bath, how they radiated warmth like little heaters. His heart squeezed as he tucked them back in, listening to their murmurs as he gently moved them.

He stood for a moment, looking at them, feeling the almost unbearable pang of a love so deep he couldn't find words for it. His sons. His gift from Mary. Her legacy.

Then, reluctantly, he headed back downstairs to deal with his unexpected visitor. Or maybe to be dealt with himself, depending.

The coffee was just finishing up, and he pulled out two mismatched mugs. "Milk? Sugar?"

"Black is fine," she answered.

After filling the mugs, he once again had to face her. Pretty enough, although she looked thin, and somewhat austere. Blond hair had been pulled severely back as if it were a nuisance she just wanted out of her way. She'd unbuttoned her coat, revealing jeans and a blue sweater that nearly matched her smoky blue eyes.

He placed the mugs on the table, one in front of her, then sat, facing her across the expanse of aging oilcloth. The pattern was bright, ripe cherries with stems on a white background. Chosen by Mary and in sad need of replacement as it had begun to crack. Somehow he couldn't let go of it.

Then he waited, because he was damned if he was going to open the can of worms himself.

After a moment, she sighed. He watched her stuff her hand into a pocket in her coat and she opened a thin badge case, laying out her ID on the table for him to see.

"Like I said, NCIS. I'm not supposed to be here, but I've got questions, I need answers and the worst you can do is tell me to go to hell. I've survived worse."

He sat back a little, studying the badge and the identification card, then looking at her. "Why don't you just get to the point?"

"Good idea." Her tone grew brisk, professional. "I knew Mary fairly well. She worked for us."

At that Dom's heart slammed. "Now, wait. She was a *nurse*."

"True. She was a nurse. A damn fine nurse. Part of her ostensible mission was what we call 'winning hearts and minds.' She told you about that, I'm sure."

He nodded. He'd been so proud of her for that.

"So twice a week, every week, she'd go into this Iraqi town and work with the women and their daughters on health issues. I'm not sure how much you know about sharia, which is Islamic law, but these women couldn't be tended by male doctors."

"I know."

Courtney nodded. "So okay. Mary was a nurse practitioner. She could deal with most of the day-to-day stuff, and she even developed a network of female physicians she could call on for advice or to take cases she couldn't handle herself. The women grew really fond of her."

"She took a lot of pride in that."

"I know she did. And because of that, when we discovered there was a problem, she agreed to work with us."

"Work with you how?"

"We got wind that some of our guys were raping and intimidating these women into silence. We couldn't prove it. The women wouldn't talk. So we asked Mary to keep her ear to the ground."

That certainly sounded like Mary. "She'd have gotten all steamed up about that."

"To put it mildly." A faint smile lifted one corner of Courtney's mouth. "She really believed that line from that song she was always humming. You know the one." She hummed a few bars.

Indeed he did. He closed his eyes against a sudden spear of grief, then quickly opened them again. Any doubt he might have harbored that this woman knew Mary vanished. In spite of himself, he leaned forward, resting his elbows on the table. "Did she find out something?"

"I think she may have, but I don't know for certain. She called me and we agreed to meet for coffee at this little local place we both liked. I thought our meetings looked innocent enough. But just the day before…"

When she trailed off, he filled in the blank. And he forced himself to say the words. "She was killed in an ambush."

"Yes."

"Well, I don't know if she knew anything. She never mentioned any of this to me."

"She wouldn't."

"Then why—" He broke off as it clicked. Icy shock poured through him, leaving him feeling almost light-headed. "You think she was *murdered?*"

Her mouth tightened, her gaze lowered. He read her answer in her reluctance.

The simmering rage that he almost rid himself of had begun to heat again with her arrival, and now it began to glow hotter. But initial shock kept it from becoming a conflagration. He had to be sure. "You're not saying she was killed by the enemy."

At last she lifted her gaze and looked him straight in the eye. "The area was pacified. She usually traveled in a small convoy to town, but that day there was only the truck she was in. And she was the *only* person killed or wounded in that ambush."

He jumped up from the table, knocking his chair over. The crash made him wince. The boys…. But even thoughts of them couldn't still him now. He began pacing, his hands flexing with a need to break something. Anything. Anger rose like a force of nature, an anger he hadn't felt since the VA had initially refused to give Mary a Purple Heart because she was officially a noncombatant.

He needed to pound something, smash something. He whirled on the woman who had brought this new horror into his life. "Are you sure?" He practically hissed the words.

"No."

That word stopped him in his tracks. What the hell? His fury transferred to her, but before he could react to it, she continued speaking.

"I believe that ambush was planned. I believe Mary was killed by the people we were looking for. I believe it all the way to my soul. But when I tried to investigate, they stopped me and sent me home. I tried again while I was at Camp Lejeune and they stopped me yet again. Told me to leave desert ghosts alone, it wouldn't do any good."

"Then what are you doing here?"

She looked down again, but this time when she raised her gaze, he could see her eyes were damp. "Because I think your wife was a hero, Mr. Mason. A true hero. I believe she died trying to protect women and girls who couldn't protect themselves. You should know that. And you should know that one way or another I'm going to find out who did this to her. It's my fault she put her life on the line, and I want you to know that she hasn't been forgotten. And I'm going to make damn sure she didn't die in vain."

A minute or more passed in utter silence. Then, feeling as if every muscle in his body were lead, he crossed the kitchen, picked up his chair, and sat. What else could he do?

Nothing, he told himself, had really changed. Mary was still gone, had been gone for two years. How and why hardly seemed relevant now that he'd adjusted to the fact that his wife, a nurse, had been a casualty of war. Nothing had changed, except possibly the vague identity he'd assigned to the person who had pulled the trigger. How did that matter now?

Numbness began to replace fury. Hardly aware of what he was doing, he lifted his coffee mug and drank.

Courtney spoke. "She was a real hero."

"She was a hero to me all along."

He saw her face pale a shade. "That's true. I just mean she went above and beyond…."

"She went above and beyond every time she went to that town to take care of those women. Every time she left the security of her hospital. Hell, she went above and beyond when she put on that uniform."

"True." Courtney appeared unable to bear his gaze right now. Not that he could blame her. Numb or not, he was probably still shooting fire from his burning eyes.

"So what," he finally asked between clenched teeth, "is your point in coming here?"

She shook her head, appearing a bit overcome, and he gave her space to collect herself. He somehow suspected this woman was rarely at a loss for words or arguments, but she seemed to be right now.

"I came," she said slowly, "for a couple of reasons. Yes, your wife was a hero. But she was more of a hero than you know. She risked her life to tend our wounded troops. She risked her life to go into a potentially hostile town to deliver medical care to women and girls who would get it no other way. But *those* risks were part of wearing the uniform. She knew it, she did it, and that's plenty for you to be proud of."

"But?"

"But she was also willing to go beyond that, to risk her life in a way that wasn't even remotely in her job description. A way she didn't have to. A way she could have said no to. She did it because she couldn't stand the thought that women were being terrorized, and she did it even knowing she might put herself in serious jeopardy. She did it because I asked her to."

"So this is all about you feeling guilty?"

"Partly. I admit it." Her eyes looked red. "I was just doing my job, but she did *more* than hers. I want justice for her, and for all those women."

"But they stopped you?"

"More than once. I don't know if they're more worried that I might find the evildoers or if they're more concerned about bad publicity. Basically, if I keep pushing this I can probably kiss my career goodbye."

"But you're still pushing."

"Yes."

He felt an unwilling flicker of respect for her. "Even though it might cost you everything."

"It won't cost me more than my job. It's a paltry price compared to the one Mary paid, that you and your sons have paid."

He couldn't argue with that. And he was furious. Furious that all of this was being raked up again, that this woman was twisting his perception of what had happened to his wife from one of an accident of war to deliberate murder. It had been hard enough to live with the former.

He had sat here any number of times with one of Mary's friends. He'd listened, he'd tried to soothe, he'd heard stories he wished he had never heard. He had offered comfort to people who had come to comfort him but who had turned out to need it every bit as much as he did. People who had been inalterably changed by their experiences over there, leaving him sometimes grateful that Mary would never have to live with those memories.

And now another one. Different, but the same. He watched her, seeing a degree of his own anguish, but worse, seeing guilt. Lots of guilt, as if she had pulled the trigger herself. If the last two years had taught him anything, it was that he couldn't do or say anything to change what this woman was feeling.

She had to deal with her demons in her own way, in her own time. Clearly, coming here was part of her dealing, regardless of the reasons she offered. Regardless of the pain it reawakened in him.

He couldn't hate her for that, or even blame her. Mary was still gone regardless. All he could do was to help make one of her former comrades feel a little better. Maybe ease a nightmare or two.

"Stay the night," he said.

"No, I couldn't possibly impose."

"You're not imposing. I've got a guest room all made up, hardly ever use it anymore. One thing for sure is I'm not letting you drive back alone down these dark roads at this hour. If you have a breakdown, it's likely no one would come along before morning. We go to bed early in these parts."

"My car is fine."

"And you're not. Just stay so I don't have to sit up worrying. In the morning…" He hesitated. "In the morning I can let you go through the stuff I saved for the boys. Emails, letters, some videotapes. I don't have everything. Some of it was too personal. I never wanted the boys to see it. But I've still got most of it."

He didn't miss the way her gaze brightened. Not enough to tick him off, but enough to let him know she'd been hoping for a little cooperation from him.

Of course she had. She had a nightmare to put to bed, and the answer might be in Mary's things.

He might have grown mad again, but his capacity for anger had lessened with time. As if he'd burned out so much of it all he could do was simmer, and his flare-ups were limited in scope and duration. He'd lived with the unanswered questions for a long time now: Why Mary? Why her, why that moment, that place? There were no answers, at least none he'd ever gotten. It was war. No other answer.

But this woman was seeking a different answer. He doubted any answers she found would do him any good, one way or another at this point. But they might do her some good.

And finding good in much these days was like trying to wring blood from stone.

"You got a suitcase?"

"Yes."

"Then let's go get it and I'll show you the room. Need anything to eat?"

"I'm fine."

He doubted it. But he wasn't fine, either.

Chapter 2

Courtney barely noticed the guest room and hall bath. She had driven almost straight through from Georgia, she was still on east coast time, and for her that meant it was nearly 1:00 a.m.

She should have fallen straight to sleep, but instead she was restless, dealing with the unexpected storm that had hit her the instant she saw Dom. God, he looked good enough to eat. She'd never felt that kind of instant attraction to a man, where her body wanted to melt the instant she clapped eyes on him.

And she hated herself for it. He was Mary's husband. She'd come here to do a job, nothing else. And damn it, she should never have accepted his offer to stay. Awareness of him, so instant, unexpected and overwhelming, seemed to hang around her now that she was staying in his house.

She should have gotten the hell out as quickly as she gracefully could and found a motel. Somewhere she wouldn't be lying awake wondering if she'd lost her mind, if she'd been alone too long or what?

Because a man's appearance shouldn't have struck her that way. It never had before. Damn, it was a wonder she hadn't sat there drooling. And the waves of shame that washed over her were almost enough to make her weep.

Rolling over, she pounded the pillow a couple of times as if she could make it softer. Tomorrow. She'd stick out one day and then leave before she did something she'd feel guilty about forever. With that resolution, she finally fell into a sleep disturbed by nightmares that never left her anymore. Nightmares of unbearable heat, mutilated bodies and screams.

Morning arrived in twilight, early it seemed, but she could hear voices downstairs, and the wonderful aroma of cooking bacon. Her mouth started watering almost before her eyes opened. How long had it been since she had allowed herself a strip of bacon?

She heard the light patter of young boys' voices, answered by the deeper tones of their father. The sounds were as inviting as the smells, and she hopped out of bed, heading for the bathroom.

She'd barely noticed last night, but she noticed this morning: the bathroom was spotless, as if awaiting a white-glove inspection. It struck her, because this was a bachelor household now, and most bachelors she knew didn't care much about such things.

But as she walked downstairs, she noted that the entire house seemed to be orderly and spotless, far more than her own apartment and she thought *she* was a clean freak.

Entering the kitchen, she found the twins sitting at the oak table and Dominic standing at the stove, frying eggs. The boys immediately fell silent, and Dom turned. His smile seemed small but natural enough.

"Boys, this is Ms. Tyson. She knew your mom."

The boys surprised her by pushing back from the table and politely standing. "Hi, I'm Kyle," said one and his clone said, "I'm Todd. Nice to meet you."

Kyle bounced around the table to hold a chair out for her and she sat. Two pairs of dark eyes, very like their dad's, stared at her.

"Your mom showed me pictures of you," she ventured. "I always asked how she could tell you apart."

Kyle scoffed. "She never had a problem. We're not *exactly* the same. Dad can tell us apart, too."

"That doesn't keep you from trying to fool me," Dom remarked, which got him a pair of laughs.

There was already a hefty platter of bacon on the table, and now Dom brought her a cup of coffee. She reached for it, holding it in both hands as she tried to figure out how to talk to the boys. She didn't have a lot of experience with kids.

Todd spoke. "Lots of Mom's friends came to visit. I guess they liked her a lot."

"I certainly liked her. And I admired her. Your mom was a hero." She saw Dom's back stiffen as he stood at the stove, and realized he feared she might get into her purpose in coming. She felt a moment of annoyance that he might think she was that insensitive, then reminded herself he didn't know her at all, and she *had* come barging into his life with an upsetting story and no prior warning.

"Yeah," said Kyle. "We have her medals. And a flag."

A pretty pathetic substitute, Courtney thought, then looked down for fear her face might give away her darkening thoughts.

She was saved by the arrival of a platter of cheesy scrambled eggs on the table, and as soon as Dom sat, the platters began to move her way. She took a slice of buttered toast, a strip of bacon and a spoonful of eggs, trying not to think about cholesterol.

"You don't eat much," Kyle remarked.

"I don't work as hard as you guys do." Safe assumption, she supposed, although at her last physical the doctor had told her to gain some weight, that she'd slipped far enough for it to be a concern.

It wasn't as if she was trying to lose weight. She just didn't feel like eating much anymore. This whole thing with Mary gnawed at her like a hungry shark.

Conversation came to a halt as two ravenous boys ate, then jumped up to grab jackets and backpacks. She watched as Dom made sure they had everything.

"I'm going to take them to the bus stop," he told her. "Back in about twenty minutes."

She watched them go out the back door and felt an ache she couldn't quite explain to herself. She had never been interested in the whole marriage and family thing. Not ever. All her life she'd been oriented toward other goals, and toward her career.

But she ached anyway at the sight of a big, strong man ushering two small boys gently out the door to catch a school bus.

Man, she was losing it.

Losing it enough that she helped herself to a second strip of bacon and another spoonful of eggs. Damn the cholesterol anyway. Enough was enough.

And *enough* was the entire reason she was here. She had helped lead Mary to her death, and she wasn't willing to let the culprits go free. No way.

Dom returned in twenty minutes as he'd promised. His booted feet clomped on the mudroom floor as he doffed his jacket and hung his keys on a wall hook. He gave her another reserved smile and a nod before he went to freshen his coffee.

He was such an attractive man, attractive in a way she wasn't used to: weather and work hardened, lean-muscled, not bulked up. And there was the easy way he walked across the kitchen, a man at home in his body.

She supposed she should feel guilty for even noticing. Guilty for a helpless, unwanted sexual response.

"I should clear up the dishes," she said, feeling awkward about imposing again.

"Naw, it'll keep. If you don't want any more, I need to add it to the compost."

"You made enough for an army," she tried to joke.

A flicker of humor danced across his face. "Those two kids usually eat like one. And I made a bit extra because I don't know your appetite."

"Not usually good. But I enjoyed breakfast. So…do you have a lot of work to do? Ranching must be loaded with it."

"It is. Less at the moment than other times of year, but yeah, I've got plenty to do. After you finish your coffee, I'll introduce you to the rest of the family."

"The rest?"

"The horses, of course. And a handful of dogs who seem to prefer equine company to human."

"I can sympathize with the dogs."

"Me, too, a lot of the time."

A smile flickered across his face again, and brief though it was, it lit him from within. She couldn't imagine the world he lived in, the way he must view things compared to her, but whatever his ranch life was like, sorrows aside, it seemed to have given him some kind of ineffable…understanding? Peace?

Crazy thinking, she told herself. Last night she had seen him furious. This was no Zen monk living above it all or beyond the reach of life's misfortunes. Yet this morning he seemed quiet within himself, a state of mind she could only envy.

Maybe it was just the early hour.

He startled her by looking her over suddenly, as if measuring her. Before she could instinctively draw back, he said, "Do you have any jeans with you?"

"Yes."

"And socks. A good pair?"

"I'm a jogger. I buy good socks."

"Well, go get on some jeans and socks, then. I'll find you a pair of boots, and then we'll go out to meet the herd. Shoe size?"

"Nine."

He nodded. "I can do that."

So she went back upstairs and pawed through her suitcase, pulling out some faded jeans, a sweatshirt and a windbreaker she'd stuffed into a corner of her suitcase at the last minute. She didn't think her long wool coat would be suitable for meeting his horses. She almost laughed at the thought.

When she came back down, he had a pair of rubber boots ready for her. "This way if you step in something we can hose you off."

She hadn't thought about that part, but she wasn't squeamish by nature. If she had been, she wouldn't have survived her job for long.

They exited the house through the mudroom into a crisp morning and warm light from the still-rising sun. He paused, using his arm to point things out.

"Arena and barn over there. I don't usually need to stable the horses unless there's a problem of some kind."

She looked at the buildings, the barn an identifiable shape with a gambrel roof, the arena obviously the big round, weathered building. She glanced toward the pasture where she could see horses by the dozens if not a hundred. "How could you stable so many anyway?"

"They don't need stabling. But a good number of them will be sold next month. Too bad you can't be here for the shindig."

"What kind of shindig?"

"I'll probably have about forty buyers here, maybe more. They'll come in RVs mostly, and I've even got power hookups for them out thataway." He pointed. "This place is going to look like a campground on steroids, or even some kind of fair."

She looked around trying to imagine it. There were two huge corrals, neither one of them occupied by a horse at present. All the horses were farther away, in what she assumed was a pasture.

"Is the arena for the buyers?"

"Yup, and for training. We put the horses through their paces one at a time in the arena, and interested folks can watch and come down to check on them more closely. Then we spend most of the winter on training."

"How many will you sell?"

A quiet laugh escaped him. "That's always the question, isn't it? I hold back my youngsters unless I'm sure they'll be handled properly."

"What do you mean?"

"You can cut five years off a horse's working life by overworking her during the first four or five years. I don't like that."

She looked at him, feeling a twinge of real respect. "That makes it harder on you, doesn't it? All those extra years of looking after them?"

"Well, I won't have to hold back many. I know the folks I invite to my sale, and most of them agree with my philosophy. I'm not saying you can't work a young horse, but overwork is another matter. So I choose to let them go to buyers I can trust. It makes them healthier. It makes them better and happier. I don't just own them, you know. I'm a steward."

She nodded, liking his attitude. "So exactly how does this work? You keep the babies until they're grown enough? You train them?"

He shook his head. "I keep a certain number for myself but I sell a lot of my mares while they're in foal for the second or third time. That means they're pregnant. But I make darn sure I know who I'm selling them to. Most folks want a good mare already in foal because they can get an idea of the quality of the foal from the mare, and because the mare is a proven breeder. It's all about quality, and folks who respect quality are going to take good care of that foal."

"Okay." They were walking toward the pasture fence now, past the corrals. The horses began to take note of them, and there was a slow but steady gathering in the general direction of the fence where a huge wooden box sat just outside. "And the rest?"

"I keep most of my geldings to train, some to show. I can sell them to stables, to rodeos, to ranches, places where they don't want to do the hard work of initial training. It takes a lot of work to train these horses to be the kind of animal you want. And of course I keep my best mares for breeding, and a handful of youngsters for showing. Have to keep my bloodline in good condition."

"It all sounds complicated." She glanced his way and saw his face, shadowed by the brim of his cowboy hat. He smiled faintly as he looked out toward the horses.

"Only if you aren't familiar with it."

"Still, it sounds like you have to weigh a lot of things."

"I suppose so. But I've been weighing them for so long it kind of happens in the background."

She looked out toward the pasture again, at the coalescing herd. "So most of them will be gone in a month?"

"That's always the question. The word I'm most focused on is *enough*." He let out a piercing whistle, and most of the horses heading their way picked up their pace. Like moles popping out of the ground, three black-and-white dogs appeared, running along with them. Border collies, she thought.

When they reached the fence, he lifted the lid on the big wooden box and began to pull out carrots. "Help yourself. They love them."

She wasn't ready to do that. She hung back a bit, aware that she was being regarded suspiciously by dozens of equine eyes even as they edged toward Dom for their treats. He seemed to enjoy handing out the carrots, and even gave one to each of the dogs.

"Dogs eat carrots?" The notion amazed her. She'd never had a dog, and mentally she associated them with bowls of dog food and scraps from the table. Which, she decided, made it rather silly of her to be surprised that they liked raw carrots.

"Dogs'll eat most anything. They even to try to swipe watermelon when I give it to the boys."

Watching, Courtney noticed that not all the horses came to the fence. Plenty hung back, as if interested but not hungry. Many of the hangers-back were still young-looking, coltish, and they seemed to hug the sides of mares.

After a bit, Dom stuffed some carrots in the back pockets of his jeans, closed the box and said, "Come on, let's go see how the gang is doing."

Passing that fence was a big step for her. She knew that horses were big, had even ridden a few times, and while these weren't as big as draft horses she'd seen, they were big enough in their current numbers to intimidate, especially when they seemed to be regarding her suspiciously.

Or maybe that was her imagination. Maybe they were simply curious. They didn't run away or anything. They shook their heads at her and made quiet little nickers but no threatening moves. Dom interested them more anyway.

For them he had plenty of pats and scratches and he called each by name. She couldn't imagine how he told them apart but gradually realized that for all they looked the same, they weren't.

They had different markings, sometimes subtle differences, different ways of standing and approaching Dom. They stood patiently as he lifted their feet and checked their hooves, nuzzled at his pockets for a carrot, and sometimes even nudged him gently. He always chuckled when that happened.

After a while, she began to feel more comfortable moving through the herd and apparently her comfort communicated because one mare with a light brown forelock came closer.

"That's Marti," Dom said. "She's one of my oldest mares and you want her approval."

"How do I get that?"

"Just hold still. If she comes close enough, pat her flank, not her head. Stay to her side and don't get directly in front of her."

She stood very still and waited. Marti edged closer, tossing her head in a manner that seemed almost like a greeting.

"Easy," Dom said. "I think she likes you."

Courtney wasn't as sure about that, but surprisingly enough, she felt relaxed and not at all threatened. Maybe she was picking up on the horse's energy?

At last Marti edged in until she stood only a foot away. Her big soft eye watched Courtney.

"You can pat her now," Dom said. "Don't move fast."

So Courtney slowly extended her arm and gently patted

the mare's shoulder. Marti tossed her head again and edged a little closer. The message was unmistakable. Courtney tried to imitate Dom's firm hard pats and Marti apparently liked it because she turned her head until it was behind Courtney and blew hot air between her lips before giving a quiet nicker.

Courtney felt a gentle nudge, possibly the horse's version of a pat, then Marti pulled back, tossed her head once more, and meandered away.

"Good job," Dom said. "You've been approved."

Courtney felt a silly grin spread across her face. "Why does that make me feel like a million bucks?"

"Because it should." He was smiling at her, the most natural smile she'd gotten from him, and it warmed her.

After a moment he spoke. "Okay, I've got to gather them in and check them over. That's going to take most of the day."

"Getting ready for the sale?"

"Partly. Partly it's just normal care. Some of these head just came in from summer pasture, and while I check on them often, it's not always as close and personal as I can get at this time of year. I need to move them into a pen and look them over."

"What do you want me to do?"

He hesitated. "I'll take you back to the house. You can look through that stuff of Mary's that I kept."

She had come here to do precisely that, so why did she all of a sudden feel so reluctant? Maybe because for a little while out here with the horses she'd forgotten everything else.

Smothering a sigh, casting a look back at Marti, who was still watching her, she followed Dom back to the house. He led her to a downstairs room that was clearly his office.

"I'm going to set you up on the boys' computer," he said. "It's a good one, but the other is for my business and I just don't let anyone touch it."

"I understand. I wouldn't let anyone else touch it, either."

He pulled down a letter-size file box from a shelf. "This is it. Everything's on CD, but I printed out a lot of it so the boys could look it over when they want because I'd rather not risk them messing up one of the CDs. She also sent a bunch of snapshots."

"You need backups."

"I've got it all backed up on an external hard drive, but nobody but me touches that."

She looked at him as she accepted the box. "Are you sure?"

The last of the relaxation had disappeared from his face, and she could see that he was at least as tense as she. Damn. She thought she had known what she would do to this man by coming here, but now she wondered if she had even come close to imagining the pain she was inflicting.

"The videos are on the CDs, too. I take it you know your way around a computer?"

"Intimately."

"Okay." He paused just long enough to start his sons' machine, give her a nod, and leave.

Her heart grew so heavy she couldn't face the task she'd come to do. Not immediately. Instead she went to stand on the mud porch and watch Dom.

She heard him give a whistle, a different one that he'd given earlier, and the three dogs immediately dashed his way.

"Away to me," she heard him call.

The dogs immediately separated, and she watched in amazement as they began to gather the herd, cutting back and forth, bringing the outliers in, and then gradually moving the entire group toward the east end of the pasture.

The horses didn't seem bothered in the least, as if they were accustomed to being herded by the dogs. And she noted the dogs didn't exactly seem aggressive in their behavior, just insistent.

Little by little, the herd coalesced. Then the dogs changed strategy. When Dom whistled and pointed, they began to line up all those horses so that soon they were filing toward the pen to the northeast. Amazing. She could have stood and watched all day.

Especially since it had been a long time since she had noticed an attractive man in this way. And he *was* attractive. Guilt pierced her again as she felt the unmistakable prickling of sexual interest. No. Not Mary's husband. Talk about betrayal.

She was dragging her heels, she realized. She didn't want to dive into Mary's past, didn't want to taste the sorrow once again. Didn't want to be reminded of all that had been destroyed by a sniper's bullet.

God, she still had nightmares about it, moments when she would simply freeze up, imagining how it had all played out. And she hadn't even been there. She looked at the box full of Mary's memories, the memories that were all her children and husband had left, and she felt a burst of self-hatred. But for her genius suggestion, Mary would probably still be here. Out there even now helping her husband with the horses.

But she didn't know how much time she had. Dom might give her another night here, but there was no reason to expect he'd want her around tomorrow. He was a busy man, and she was a reminder of bad things. Things he probably couldn't afford to think about too often.

Things she needed to take care of so they would stop haunting *her*.

She understood him. Oh, she definitely understood that much.

Outside, Dom walked down to the pen where he was going to process the horses one at a time. Ted, his only full-time help, was already waiting.

Times had changed enough that he could no longer afford to keep a full-time staff of hands to help him out, but all the local ranches were suffering to one degree or another, so they shared their hired help. Today he'd have three or four guys he knew well from a couple of his neighbors' places. One of these days, he promised himself he was going to do well enough again to keep a couple more hands on permanently. In fact, judging by the response to his recent invitation to the sale, he might be right on the cusp of becoming one of the best breeders around.

It was his goal. When he'd been very young, and Granddad had run the ranch, selling horses had been simpler. Cowboys hadn't yet faded into the mists of memory, rodeos had been more popular, and horses hadn't been entirely about breeds and bloodlines. Good workers had been what most people wanted.

As times had changed, though, he had changed with them. A lot of his stock now was show stock, the kind people bought to strengthen their own herds in order to win prizes because those prizes meant good stud fees. He showed some of his own horses every winter and had gotten enough recognition that his line was doing well.

He still had his regular customers, too, everything from guest ranches, to rodeos, to people who just liked horses and could afford to keep a stable. Sometimes he even thought about branching out into draft horses, Belgians maybe, because there was a pretty firm market for horses that could pull wagons, sleighs and carriages.

So far his quarter horses hadn't made a big showing on the race circuit, but they were getting closer. He had mixed feelings about that, so he was reluctant to push in that direction.

He paused, just before he reached the pen, aware that the horses were steadily closing in from behind at the dogs' urgings. Ted gave him a quizzical look.

Why was he thinking about this right now? His business plan was pretty clear, and so far seemed to be working well enough that he was able to keep the ranch and keep his sons' futures bright.

He was just distracting himself, he realized. Trying not to notice the anxiety churning in the pit of his stomach because that bit of a woman had walked through his door and opened up all the barely healed wounds once again.

She was kind of pretty, but he would have thought her a whole lot prettier if she weren't so thin. The way she'd pecked at breakfast this morning had been disturbing. He wondered if she was one of those health-food nuts.

People like that always made him shake his head a bit. Of course, as Mary had always said, "If folks worked hard enough or exercised enough, they wouldn't have to worry about everything they put in their mouths."

True, he supposed. His family had always worked hard on this ranch, and most of them had lived to a very ripe old age. Right now he should have been working alongside his dad and granddad, and would have been except for an accident on an icy mountain road eight years ago.

Cripes. He caught himself, wondering why he couldn't stay away from the paths of grief and loss. He'd made peace with all that. It was the way of life. *All* life.

Relief filled him as he heard the sounds of an approaching truck engine. His help was arriving, and now they'd be so busy he wouldn't have time to think.

No time to think of lost family and wife, no time to try to avoid noticing that Courtney was appealing in a way he'd never thought he'd feel again.

Thinking had become an enemy of sorts. Something to be dodged unless it was squarely focused on work or the boys.

Well, he had plenty to do today and that would prevent him from having to play hide-and-seek inside his own head.

Thank God.

Chapter 3

The boys came home from school between three and four. Evidently they must have a rather long bus ride. Courtney heard their return with relief, because other than an offer of lunch she had skipped, she had spent the day being a voyeur in the life of a dead friend.

It hurt. She felt guilty. But she also felt envious. Mary's emails to her sons had been both beautiful and touching, and incredibly upbeat. Given that Mary's days had been almost entirely devoted to dealing with the ugly consequences of the worst side of human nature, the tone of her communications was remarkable. She always found some cute and funny story to tell the boys, often about a dog some of the hospital members had adopted.

Courtney knew that adoption was officially frowned upon. Dogs in Iraq were considered unclean animals, and lived out their short and pathetic lives as scavengers who were often kicked and otherwise mistreated. Soldiers naturally wanted to save them, but official policy forbade it. Many rescued dogs were ordered killed if commanders found out about it.

So the tales of how the hospital managed to keep and hide a dog were filled with life, laughter and even a touch of amusingly wicked pleasure.

Another insight into Mary, one that made Courtney like her even more. And miss her even more.

An insight her sons would cherish more as they grew older.

But whatever Courtney had hoped to find, she quickly divined that she would not find it in emails to the boys. That left copies of their Skype conversations, photographs and any videos Mary might have mailed home.

By the time the boys returned from school, she was quite certain she was not up to viewing them. Not today. Not after the emotional morass she had hiked through in reading those emails. Seeing Mary's maternal side made her acutely aware, as never before, of just what the twins had lost and would now never know.

She was just about to shut down her computer, but decided to check her email first. She had a few friends who might be wondering where she had gone, and she probably needed to assure them she was really just on a vacation, far, far away.

And indeed the first several were exactly what she expected, friendly demands to know where she was, requests for a photo or two, declarations of envy.

But the fourth in the list came from an address she didn't recognize. Thinking it must be junk mail her filter hadn't caught, she clicked on it, wondering why it hadn't been shuffled to the correct folder.

What she found made her neck prickle.

I know what you're up to. If you think you can get away with it, you're wrong. I'm watching you.

Her heart slammed, and she could barely breathe. She'd felt the implied threat before, but always so subtly she had been able to think she was imagining it. Those orders to stop investigating had always been couched in reasonable terms, making it impossible to say for certain that there was any intended threat.

But there was no mistaking that email. A shiver trickled down her spine, but then she reminded herself that no way on earth could anyone know she was here. Before leaving, she'd made noises about going to the Pacific Northwest to enjoy a cooler climate and some time on the water. Heck, she'd even left a couple of brochures on her desk.

No. No one could know she was here. Absolutely no one.

Fear and shock quickly gave way to anger. Using the skills she had learned on her job, she tried to trace the email's origin, and found it came from an anonymous account in Finland. Damn, she hated those things. They were virtually impossible to break through.

Finally, disgusted, she deleted the mail and shut down the machine. Her self-control back in place, she got up from the computer, packed up the emails and the CDs and went out to the kitchen where she heard the voices. The boys were already diving into an after-school snack.

As she entered the room, Dom said to them, "I've got another twenty horses to do, and then I'll be done for the day and we'll start dinner. Be sure to get going on that homework."

"Okay," came a pair of answers.

Dom saw Courtney and looked at her. The quietude had come back to his dark eyes, and it didn't waver when he saw her. "You must be hungry by now. Ask the boys what's handy. I need maybe another hour with the horses."

"Thanks."

He gave her the briefest of nods, clapped his hat back on his head and strode out the back door.

Kyle got her an apple and she joined them at the table.

Todd asked, "You got any kids?"

"No."

"Are you gonna stay for a while?"

"I don't think so. Maybe another day." She wondered why the boys exchanged looks at that, but decided maybe they were relieved to know life would go back to normal soon.

And it *was* possible to tell them apart, she realized. There was the slightest difference in their noses, a small hint of a downturn at the corners of Kyle's eyes. Not something to be noticed at a glance. And Todd had a very tiny mole on his left cheek. "I can tell you apart!" she announced with surprise.

That caused both boys to shriek with laughter. "They put us in separate classes cuz the teachers have trouble."

"Let me guess. I bet you sometimes switch."

They shifted, their guilty looks answer enough. Courtney laughed. "And I bet you don't help them out at all."

Kyle shrugged. "Why should we? All they have to do is really look at us."

Courtney couldn't really argue against that. Even if playing jokes and switching classes wasn't a good thing to be doing. And that caused her to think of something else. "Does it bother you that they don't look?"

Apparently they hadn't thought of it in those terms before. And why should they, given their youth? Replies were slow in coming, almost as if they wondered if there was a right answer. Or as if they weren't sure how they felt.

"I guess, sometimes," Kyle said eventually. "Mostly it seems funny." He glanced at Todd. "Right?"

"Mostly," Todd agreed. "But sometimes it's not so funny."

"Like when?"

"Like…like when we can switch classes for a whole day and nobody notices."

Courtney's heart twinged. "Does it make you feel invisible?"

Todd shrugged. Apparently the waters were getting too deep for a seven-year-old. "I dunno. It just isn't funny sometimes."

"I guess I can see that." And she could. "But you know what?"

"What?"

"You have different fingerprints, even though you're twins."

The boys perked up at that. "So we couldn't get mixed up for real?"

"No way."

"Can you take our fingerprints?"

"I don't have a kit with me. But if it's okay with your dad, I think your sheriff could do it and give them to you."

All of a sudden, both boys were grinning again, happier in some way. Funny, she had always thought twins liked being twins, but faced with these two it occurred to her that being a twin might have impacts that had never occurred to her. Something to keep in mind.

As ordered, they dived into their homework, which amounted to a couple of worksheets that didn't take too long. They wanted Courtney to supervise, so after warning them that it had been a long time since second grade for her and she might not remember enough to be useful—which got more giggles—she sat between them and helped when requested. Which wasn't often, because these boys seemed to have a good understanding of what they were doing.

They were just finishing up when Dom returned. Courtney turned to join the boys in their greeting and noted the way he appeared to be arrested, as if something in the sight of the three of them gave him pause.

At once Courtney realized she might appear to be taking Mary's place. She started to rise, but Dom waved her to stay.

"I need a shower," he said shortly. "Back in ten."

She watched him walk from the room, listened to the sound of his feet on the stairs.

Be careful, she reminded herself. Be careful. The man was a grieving widower, and her mere presence in the house had to be uncomfortable for him, never mind her mission.

The boys appeared oblivious to any undercurrents, however. They finished the last bit of their worksheets, tucked them in folders and away in their backpacks.

Then, like a pair of small whirlwinds, they grabbed their jackets and darted out the door, calling to her to come with them because they wanted to see the horses.

At once she jumped up, hunting for the boots she had worn that morning, grabbing her own windbreaker from a hook. The idea of those two little boys alone out there with those large horses didn't seem exactly safe.

By the time she got out there, the two of them were perched on the fence rail looking absolutely comfortable and confident. A few of the horses had come over to take carrots from them, and the boys reached out to stroke, scratch and pet, their touches obviously welcome.

Watching in amazement, she remembered her own initial nervousness that morning, and realized she knew nothing, absolutely nothing, about growing up on a ranch and what that evidently meant.

Those boys knew these horses, were comfortable with them and the horses appeared to reciprocate. Indeed, the twins' entire manner had changed, becoming quieter and more like their father than they had been in the house. Even their voices had softened.

Amazed and curious, Courtney walked slowly over to the fence and stood nearby. Part of her longed to be able to sit on the rail, too, and pass out carrots, but part of her was still reluctant. Oh, she had ridden horses before in her life. Every girl who could manage it did so, even if only for a short time. It wasn't as if she was afraid to *ride* a horse. A nice tame beast already saddled, with an experienced horseman there to guide her every step of the way.

This was different, and she wondered why. Because there were so many of them? Because to some extent they appeared to be wild, rather than tame, since they were out there free of all halters and saddles?

Maybe. Yet as she had just seen this morning, these horses were as tame as could be. She took a halting step toward the pasture fence, then threw back her shoulders and walked over to stand by the boys.

Todd greeted her at once and handed her a couple of carrots. "Just hold it out and see who takes it."

So, leaning against the rail, she did exactly that. Much to her amazement, a gangly-looking small horse came over, his soft lips barely touching her fingers as he took a carrot.

"Wow!" she said quietly. "That was amazing."

Todd laughed. "It's fun. They're all good horses. Dad says that's cuz we treat 'em well."

"We treat 'em like *horses*," Kyle corrected.

"Meaning?" Courtney asked as she handed out another carrot.

"They don't think like us. They need different things." Kyle sounded like he was parroting Dom, and he probably was. "Dad's teaching us all about it."

"That's great," Courtney agreed. "You're lucky. I don't know anything about horses, really."

"Dad'll take care of that. Unless you leave tomorrow."

Unless she left tomorrow. She'd been ready to do that not so long ago, as she had been reading Mary's emails and letters and learning to know a warm and wonderful side of the woman she had never met in Iraq.

But that anonymous threat, at first so shocking, seemed to have stiffened her spine. No way could she have gotten to this level in her job if a mere anonymous email could scare her off.

And somehow standing here with Mary's boys and looking out over a sunny pasture full of horses, Courtney found herself wishing she didn't have to go so soon. This place could grow on her, she realized. Seriously grow on her.

She caught herself and shook the thought away. She was falling for an image, she reminded herself. A pastoral scene that might have come out of a storybook. She hadn't the least idea how much work this place required, or how much it took out of the family. How much those beautiful horses really needed.

What she must do was keep reminding herself that she was wearing rubber boots. Even on a beautiful horse ranch, you could step in manure.

After the boys were tucked in, Dom came back downstairs almost reluctantly. He'd been aware all day of Courtney's presence on the ranch, the presence of a *woman* in the empty space left by Mary's absence.

It made him uneasy. He'd gotten used to living alone, living with hours of silence, living without companionship. And, whether he wanted to think about it or not, he felt guilty for being so aware of Courtney. Logically he knew that life went on, that he was just a man, and a man had needs. Logically he knew that Mary wouldn't want him to live out his life alone.

Hell, she'd even told him so before she shipped out. He hadn't wanted her to speak the words, had even tried to stop her, but she'd insisted on saying them anyway. "If anything happens to me, Dom, you've got to move on. For yourself and for the twins."

But his heart told a different story, as if the mere act of noticing that Courtney was a woman, a too-skinny woman even, was a betrayal of Mary.

Talk about a screwed-up head.

Right now he couldn't even summon a work-related excuse to escape into his office or escape to the barn. No, he worked so hard to avoid thinking that sometimes he couldn't come up with a single thing left to do.

Tonight was one of those nights. The paperwork was all up to date, the horses had been taken care of, the dogs fed, the dishes done. He didn't even need to clean, since he'd already washed down the tub and bathroom after bathing the boys.

And maybe the real thing that troubled him was the fear that if he sat down with Courtney he might learn that she had discovered something today, something that supported her theory that Mary had been murdered.

Right now he wasn't sure he could handle that.

Courtney sat in the living room on the sofa where he'd left her, cup of coffee on the table at her elbow. She appeared wan, he realized, as if she wasn't any less tired or any more happy about this situation than he was.

That made him uncomfortable, and it took him a minute to realize what was going on: he liked having her here. He liked the distraction, the awareness that he was still a man.

Mentally he swore some words he would never speak in the presence of the boys, and wondered if he was going off his rocker or something.

The *only* thing that should be concerning him was whether Courtney had found out something.

The words escaped his mouth before he knew they were coming. "Did you find out anything?"

"No."

"Much more to look at?"

She sighed, and he saw a glimmer of his own grief in her face. "Yes. Unfortunately. If it won't kill you to have me around another day."

"Won't kill me." Hardly that. Maybe having her around for a few days would make him face up to some stuff it suddenly occurred to him that he'd been avoiding. Stuff like maybe he needed to get on with a life apart from horses and the boys, just like Mary had told him.

Maybe his hermitage was comfortable for him, but judging by the way Kyle and Todd chattered at Courtney, it wasn't enough for them. Heck, they'd even wanted her to read them a bedtime story, a request he'd nipped upstairs because he wasn't sure he wanted them to have that intimacy with her. After all, she was moving on.

And maybe he was being terribly unfair to his sons. That caused a shaft of guilt to hit him in the gut. Here he thought he was protecting them and caring for them, when maybe he was cutting them off from things they just naturally needed.

He wouldn't do that to his horses. Was he doing that to his sons?

Slowly he settled into the easy chair facing her and tried to think of how to deal with all of this. Find a way, any way, into a conversation that might help him, or his kids, or her. Anybody.

"What exactly are you looking for?" he asked her.

"Names. Maybe faces in videos. Somebody had to be close enough to figure out that she'd found something."

"If she found something."

"If," Courtney agreed. "But I can't think of any other reason she wanted to meet with me. Once she started working for us, we pretty much stayed apart unless we came together in the usual course of things."

"So you're not like a secret agent or something."

"I'm not undercover, no. Not usually. And I knew Mary for a while before this issue ever came up. No reason to be unnecessarily covert. We'd already established a friendship that a number of people knew about."

He nodded slowly, taking in the information, trying to imagine how things must have been for Mary. He'd probably always wonder. She never talked much about Iraq, not about the ugly stuff anyway. Like she was protecting him.

"Once," he said slowly, "I tried to get her to talk about what it was like over there. She told me that when she came home on leave she wanted to recharge, not relive."

Courtney nodded. "I can hear her saying that. She had a gift, didn't she, for looking forward."

"Yup. How did you two meet?"

"Oh, I was at her hospital. There'd been an accusation from someone in supply that medical stuff was disappearing and unaccounted for. And since the Marine Corps, and by extension the navy, supplied the hospital, I was one of the people tasked to look into it."

"I thought she was at an army hospital."

"Not exactly. Units from different branches of service share the same bases and use the same facilities a lot. Everybody's got their own share of the job to do, but redundancy is expensive. Especially in hospitals. So, yes, her Guard unit was stationed there, but the hospital was being shared by everyone, and staffed by everyone. Anyway, when it came time to ask her about procedures and if she was aware of anyone stealing supplies, she gave me both barrels."

Dom chuckled. "She would do that."

"She asked me if I was an insurance company, wanting

them to account for every roll of gauze, every bandage, every aspirin."

Another chuckle escaped Dom. He could actually hear Mary speaking those words.

"Anyway," Courtney continued, "she told us in no uncertain terms that everything was being used in treatment, that sometimes they gave supplies to Iraqi medical people who were desperate, and that if we wanted to know where all that stuff was going, we needed to be there when they brought in the next load of casualties."

"Were you?"

"Yes. Sadly. And we didn't have to come back to do it. We were still there investigating when it happened. After what we saw, we went back and reported that nothing was being stolen, everything was being used. And it was, Dom. I don't know what annoyed that supply guy into making a complaint. All he had to do was leave his office and walk next door to the trauma center. The place was chaos, medical supplies were being used and discarded in huge quantities just to stabilize the patients. I don't know."

Her smoky blue gaze grew distant. "Maybe it griped him that they were treating civilians, too. If there were a lot of casualties, after they took care of their own patients, they'd grab supplies and head out to nearby Iraqi hospitals to help. It was humanitarian work, and we put in our report that in this instance they needed to call off the bean counters. Winning hearts and minds. That was part of the mission. And Mary was…well, Mary was a pure humanitarian."

"Sometimes," Dom said, hating to even admit it, "I'm glad she won't have to live with those memories."

"You should be glad," Courtney said. "If there's one blessing in any of this, it's that she *won't* have to live with that past. As good as she was, as kind as she was, she'd still have to live with the nightmare. I didn't see nearly as much of it as she did, and I still have nightmares."

He fixed his attention on her, realizing that she wasn't just some cop who had known Mary, a cop trying to do a job he wasn't yet sure he wanted her to do. In her own way, she was a vet, too. And she was a vet on a mission, whether he liked it or not. He had to respect that.

Damned if he didn't feel she needed some time to wind down. Coming out here like this had been a desperate act, he realized. Not knowing how she would be received, risking her career if it became known what she was doing, all because she couldn't let a desert ghost rest.

And that desert ghost had been his wife.

He sighed, struggling again against a torrent of emotions he'd tried to put in some isolated part of his heart simply because he had to get on with things, had to take care of two boys, couldn't afford to give in or give up.

She was stirring all that up because she couldn't lock it away as he had.

"You got any family?" he asked.

"Just my mother. We get together once or twice a year."

Maybe that explained a lot, especially about her job, which was driving her into a dangerous place. Not necessarily physically. He couldn't see any reason she should be in physical danger…unless those folks who'd been telling her to drop it might feel she was a threat.

For an instant his heart almost stopped. Had it occurred to her that whoever had killed Mary might come after her, too, if she seemed like a threat?

But then he dismissed the thought. She surely must have considered the possibility, and she'd said she was out here without telling anyone. No reason anyone should care where she took her vacation.

And whatever had happened had happened two years

ago, just another atrocity among thousands and thousands
of atrocities caused by war. However much dust and dirt she
kicked up, she was up against powers she couldn't fight solo.
What *did* seem likely to him was that she would merely put
her own neck in a career noose and make him a whole lot less
comfortable with what had happened to Mary.

He'd been through hell since her death but the picture
Courtney wanted to paint of what had happened presented
a new version of hell. One he didn't know if he could live
with.

He wasn't great with people, but he was good with horses,
and right now he felt like he was looking at a mare who was
frightened, and flailing about as she tried to figure out the
best way to respond to a goad. Goads were bad. He wouldn't
even swat a horse, and this woman looked as if she'd been
swatted good.

All he knew was the best way to handle a disturbed horse,
and heading straight at the problem was often exactly the
wrong way.

"We're going camping this weekend," he remarked. "The
boys asked if you could come." They had, but he'd put them
off, not wanting to deepen this relationship any. But that had
been his immediate response. His secondary response was the
one he always got around to sooner or later: help the horse.

She'd probably hate him if she ever figured out he was
thinking of her that way. But there it was.

"Camping?" she repeated uncertainly. "But, um…"

"You're not going to finish going through Mary's stuff
tomorrow. We both know it. And I assume, since you're
here, that you're on some kind of vacation. Because they sure
wouldn't have let you come otherwise from what you said."

"You're right."

"So take some vacation. The weather is supposed to warm
up, I need to go into the upper pasture to gather about twenty

head that are still there. The boys have a great time. We ride up on Saturday morning, gather the herd and bring them back down on Sunday."

"I...don't know."

"Think about it. I'm getting some coffee. You want fresh?"

"Please."

Just a gentle movement of the bit, he reminded himself. Just a hint to let the horse know something was needed. No woman who had gotten into her car and driven out here in defiance of her orders could be weak. No, she had to be a strong woman. But right now she was looking weak, and that was because she was floundering as she tried to find a way to deal with a burr under her saddle.

That would change, he thought. If nothing else, her visit here would convince her it was a dead end. And maybe some mountain sunshine and fresh air would clear her emotions a bit.

Because, as he'd learned these past two years, sometimes you just had to live with the way things were, like them or not.

Chapter 4

Friday morning dawned misty as the warm front moved in, bringing the possibility of light rain.

Courtney rolled onto her side and stared out the window, struck by the lack of curtains. But why would anyone need curtains here? Beyond that window lay nothing but mountains and trees. The bunkhouse, barns and main pastures were on the other side of the house and behind it. In her world, though, no window was ever left uncovered because it was too easy for people to look in from nearby buildings, or even from the ground.

A different world indeed.

From below she could hear the sounds of Dom and the boys at breakfast, and she could even smell some of the aromas that had wafted under her closed door, but not even coffee could make her move.

Emotionally, she felt trampled. Last night she had determined that she would finish up today somehow and leave.

This morning she doubted she would be able to do much of anything. It was as if a load of grief she had been carrying around, carefully compartmentalized for two years, had finally hammered her. Reading through Mary's letters to her sons had left her feeling positively battered.

Worse, it seemed to have awakened memories of things she had seen over there. Nightmares of war, of mutilated bodies, had plagued her all night. She'd awakened at least three times with the sounds of screams in her ears. But her exposure had been relatively small. Someone like Mary, someone who saw it almost every day, would surely have worse nightmares, worse memories. Worse everything.

I'm lucky, she told herself firmly. Lucky her job had taken her into hell so rarely. Other people had been there for years.

But the thought of opening those doors of memory any wider almost sickened her.

So what was she going to do? Give up her pursuit of justice? Let the desert ghosts lie in their hiding places? Because for her Mary wasn't the only ghost. So were the women of that village who had never received justice. So was the person who had murdered Mary to protect himself and his buddies. Some of those ghosts she felt unable to leave alone.

Except that today it all seemed like too much. Way too much. Her plan of poring over letters, photos and tapes had been anticipated from a professional angle. It was the kind of thing she did all the time in her job.

But this was no job. This was personal. And it hurt.

Apparently not even two years had buried the anguish completely, and she could only imagine what it was like for Dom, surrounded by all his memories of his wife, taking care of two boys who looked quite a bit like her.

Of course, maybe that had helped him deal faster than her

own burying of it had. Maybe he was further down the road than she.

Sighing, she at last rose, tended to her needs and went downstairs. Dom wasn't there and she imagined he had taken the boys to the bus. Through one of the windows she could see Ted walking out into the pastures. He appeared to be carrying some tack with him.

Breakfast still waited on the table, and the coffee was still hot and fresh. Her place had been set, as if her arrival was anticipated. Somehow that made her feel a little more welcome.

She poured some coffee and then took some pancakes and link sausages from a platter and warmed them in the microwave. Blueberry syrup topped her menu. Not that she felt much like eating. Not after the nightmares, not after that damn email yesterday that was probably as toothless as an old hag, designed to frighten her, but unable to do anything else.

She forced herself to take a bite of pancake. No, that email was meaningless. It had probably arrived simply because she had gone out of reach of oversight. And someone was worried.

Wouldn't they be horrified to realize that all they had done was confirm her suspicions that something was seriously wrong with the way the investigation had been quashed? For a moment, she almost smiled, and the taste of the pancakes became wonderful.

Yeah. They'd confirmed her suspicions. Now she would get to the bottom of this or die trying.

She tried to imagine Mary sitting at this table. All her memories of Mary involved the base, the hospital and a couple places where it was safe for an American to stop for coffee. Even in a pacified zone that wasn't always a sure thing.

She ran her fingertips over the aging oilcloth, and figured

from the pattern that it must have been Mary's choice. She had loved cheerful things.

And she probably wouldn't be very happy to see Courtney sitting here feeling as if lead weighted her down. That just wasn't Mary. She probably wouldn't be happy, either, that Courtney had gotten Dom all stirred up again.

Crap! She put her head in her hands as powerful, painful feelings grabbed her. Maybe she should have just let this lie and lived with her sense of outraged justice.

But as soon as she had the thought, she knew she couldn't rest until she was absolutely certain that she had done everything possible. *Everything.*

She heard Dom come into the mud room, and didn't even bother to look up. She didn't want to know, in a moment of reaction he couldn't conceal fast enough, how little he wanted her here.

"Are you okay?"

"No," she admitted frankly. "But it doesn't matter." And it didn't, compared to his problems.

"Of course it matters."

She listened to him pour coffee for himself, then heard a chair scrape as he sat at the table. "What's going on?"

She shook her head, still resting in her hands. "It's hard reading those emails and letters."

"I know."

Yeah, she was sure he did. And it seemed petty of her to even mention it. "How are you managing?"

He shrugged a shoulder, seeming to indicate he wasn't going to talk about it. But then he said, "With time I feel it less often. I still feel it, it still hurts like hell, but it happens less often. I guess you can get used to anything, given time."

"I guess so." She gave herself an inward shake and looked up at last, finding his strong face looking calm, even resigned. And then she caught a flicker of something else in his gaze, something hot. It was gone almost instantly, but she knew that look, had seen it often enough to know what it meant: he found her sexually attractive.

But as quickly as the heat showed, it was followed by a flash of puzzlement, as if he didn't understand what he'd just felt.

Guilt. It was thick on the air, she realized. They both felt guilty, though perhaps for different reasons. She felt it because it was partly her fault Mary had died. He probably felt that an instant of attraction somehow betrayed her. And frankly, Courtney wondered the same thing, because as she had caught that flicker of sexual yearning in his gaze, she had felt herself respond all the way to her center.

Desire, evidently, had its own calendar and its own causes, and simple thoughts of propriety, ugly things like guilt, couldn't entirely squash it.

Life went on whether you wanted it to or not. That was the hardest part. Just when you felt everything should freeze in time and space, that the whole world should halt because you had lost someone you loved, life intruded, reminding you that you had to go on.

"Have you decided whether you'll go camping with us tomorrow?" he asked.

"I…" The hesitation, so strong earlier, the decision she thought she had made…all of a sudden they were gone. "Yes. Yes, I will."

One corner of his mouth lifted. "Good. You'll enjoy it. There's a cabin up there, not much, but I've kept it up because the boys love to go up there in the summers when we look after the horses. You won't exactly be roughing it."

"It would be fun either way. I think—" she hesitated, then blurted it "—I think I need some fun."

"I think you do, too. I think we all do." His smile widened

slightly. "How devoted are you to spending another day in my office?"

She thought about all those photos she still needed to review, all the tapes and CDs. "There's a lot I need to look at still."

"Well, if it gets to be too much, come over to the arena. Ted and I are going to be working with some cutting horses today."

"Thanks, I will."

"Just don't forget your boots. We try to keep things clean outside the pastures, but we don't always get there fast enough."

That elicited a little chuckle from her, a tension breaker. His smile grew more relaxed.

"It's hard for you right now," he said.

"For *me?*"

"Yes, for you. I've been living with the memories on a daily basis for two years. You've probably gone long periods where you didn't even have time to think about it. This has all just freshened it for you."

"But not for you?"

"A bit." He sighed. "A bit. I was angry at first, but you know that."

"But not now?"

"Folks have to do what they need to do. You need to do this. Won't change much of anything for me."

But that wasn't entirely true and she knew it. He might be telling himself that, but how could it not change things for him to know his wife might have been a deliberate target rather than just someone in the wrong place at the wrong time?

She had certainly seen his anger when she first arrived, but since then she had been impressed by his steady composure, as if he had discovered a rock on which to stand, and while he might tip a bit from time to time, he recovered his balance.

She needed to do the same thing. It was a skill she had learned on other distressing cases, a way of reminding herself that the only water that wasn't over the dam was her investigation. That no matter how upsetting the crime, all she could do was seek justice.

Those cases, though, hadn't been personal. And this one might really be tipping her over the edge. She had come all this way, in defiance of orders, without sufficient thought of what she might inflict on this family. Was that a stable way to act? Was it normal to be unable to let go of her thirst for justice after two years?

Heaven knew she'd had to let go of it before, when people she had been certain were guilty had been acquitted. Not often, but it had happened. She'd learned to live with that. Was this so very different?

But she knew in her heart that it was. This was different because the investigation had been stymied, because a charge had never been laid, and a trial had never been held. All those things that she considered essential to the functioning of proper justice had been short-circuited.

And maybe that was what bothered her as much as anything. The process had been interrupted, and that wasn't right. It just plain wasn't right.

Dom was glad to get out to the arena. The atmosphere in the kitchen had grown thick, at least for him. It had been a long time since he'd felt hunger for a woman, but he felt it now. He looked at Courtney and saw a wounded mare, one who maybe didn't even know how wounded she was. He should focus on that.

Instead, when he was around her, he found his thoughts trying to ride down different trails. Trails that involved exploring those delicate curves of hers, trying to find out if she was softer than she looked, wanting to bring a hazy happiness to her eyes to replace the haunted look. And every time his mind and body wandered that way, his response was so strong it was like the air became too thick to breathe.

He hadn't felt that since he'd been with Mary, and he didn't want to feel it again. Not now. Not with a woman who was hell-bent on finding out things he wasn't sure he wanted to know. A woman who'd be leaving in a few days.

Ted had brought in a couple of the horses they were training for barrel racing. A buyer had been out a few months ago, eyed these two geldings and announced he'd buy them at the sale if they were ready to go and showed well enough.

The showing "well enough" had been the challenge. Dom trained a lot of horses, and trained them well, but these two promised a higher than ordinary price if they excelled. The buyer wanted to win competitions. It was Dom's job to ensure that he turned over two horses that could.

After that everything would depend on the buyer and his riders. But from here they were going to leave as ready winners. Maybe he'd even get to tutor the riders a bit, which would mean more money.

But even more important to him than the money in teaching the riders would be the secure knowledge that the riders would treat the horses right. Know how to handle them without making them difficult or stubborn.

Horses were happy to cooperate most of the time. As long as you didn't override their instincts, or inadvertently teach them they couldn't do anything right. And each horse had its own quirks to be handled. You could either make it into a fight, which seldom yielded the desired results, or you could make it a cooperative effort. He preferred cooperation.

These two were beautifully cooperative. He rode them both, alternately, among the barrels, at first slowly, and finally at a full gallop. They had learned to trust him, to cut around those barrels with the amazing agility of quarter horses, and there was only one minor bump on a barrel.

They were damn near ready for the buyer.

Following them, he worked with two more, younger horses, getting them used to riding the wall of the arena, cutting figure eights in smaller and smaller spaces, backing up when he leaned in the saddle.

One of the three-year-olds still didn't like the whole backing up thing, and occasionally balked. Every time he did, Dom led him away, then brought him back through the same ride, the same backup, making it clear that they would do it until the horse backed up.

And as always, eventually the youngster cooperated. With time, the repetitions needed had become fewer. It wouldn't be long before the horse stopped balking at all. He ended the workout on a success and with a lot of pats and praise.

As always, the smell of horses, sawdust and leather lifted his spirits. The sounds of their snorts, occasional whinnies and the muffled clomp of their hooves on the sawdust…all those things put him in a happy place. All his life the only thing that had ever made him happier had been Mary and the boys.

He was walking his last horse toward the door of the arena when he suddenly caught sight of Courtney sitting quietly in the back of the bleachers. He paused, surprised, wondering how long she had been there.

"Hi," he said.

"Hi. That was interesting to watch."

"Interesting to do, too. I'm about to take Jazz here to groom him and cool him a bit before I send him back to pasture. Want to come?"

"Sure." She looked almost relieved to be invited to tag along. Apparently she wasn't feeling too good by herself today.

He could understand. He'd gotten so he avoided looking through Mary's things. For a while, he'd done it almost obsessively, and then he had realized it only made him ache worse and had put everything away for the boys.

He waited while she clambered down from the bleachers and came up beside him. Jazz gave her a once-over then bobbed his head and snorted impatiently. He knew that currying awaited him and he was in no mood to stand still.

"He's a beautiful horse," Courtney remarked.

"He's got a good streak of stubborn in him, too."

She smiled. "He definitely didn't seem to like backing up."

"He has to do that based on trust because he can't see. We're working on it."

"I noticed you didn't seem to do much."

"What do you mean?"

"You were almost motionless in the saddle."

"Ah. Well, that's my training method. How I sit, what I do with my knees, whether I make his bit drop a little on one side or another. Controlling a horse isn't about force."

"I see that now."

He glanced at her, unhappy to feel once again that hot spur of desire. Damn, he didn't need this, she wasn't his type and maybe he'd just been living like a monk for too long. "Consider the size of a horse. Consider your size. Then ask who is going to win any argument."

That got a genuine laugh from her, a pretty sound that he liked. There'd been a shortage of laughter around here for too long. Oh, the boys laughed a lot, and he laughed with them, sometimes he even felt the laughter when he made the appropriate sounds. Maybe it was high time he got around to laughing more. For real.

For the sake of the boys, if nothing else.

"Maybe," he suggested, feeling oddly awkward and not

knowing why, "I should give you a few riding lessons this afternoon. For tomorrow."

"I'd like that," she said easily enough. "I've ridden a few times, but not recently, and I'm sure I don't know your methods."

"Depends. I'm not the only one who thinks this way about managing a horse. On the other hand, there are those who believe in quirts, crops, spurs, yanking the reins and just generally turning it into sheer misery for the animal."

"But you want them to trust you."

"If they don't trust me, how can I trust them? Besides, most of what I want them to do is pretty natural for them. It's just a matter of encouraging them to do it at the right time."

She nodded, looking thoughtful, and he let her be as they crossed the yard toward the barn. He'd have liked to know what she was thinking about, but didn't feel he knew her well enough to ask.

Ted met them just as they reached the barn. "You let me take care of Jazz, boss. It's lunchtime and the lady looks like she might need a bite."

Courtney surprised them both by laughing. "You sound like my doctor."

Dom glanced at Ted, wondering what was going on here. Ted knew that Dom liked to take care of horses who were being a bit difficult, another way of establishing trust. Once he'd gotten a horse that all-important point, it was okay to let someone else do the currying from time to time…hell, it was necessary with so many head. But with a horse like Jazz, Dom seldom turned over the responsibility until the horse had fully settled down.

Still, he said nothing, merely handed the lead rein to Ted and turned toward the house. He had an idea his foreman was up to something, but damned if he could read the other man's mind.

"So," he said to Courtney, "your doc is telling you to eat?"

"He's not very happy with me right now. I've always been a bit underweight, but now they're riding my case about it."

"Too much worry?"

"Maybe." She didn't quite meet his eyes, but he filled in the blanks anyway: guilt was eating her alive. He smothered a sigh, knowing there was no way possible to convince her she wasn't responsible for Mary's death. The shooter, whoever he was, took full responsibility for that.

"You know," he said as they reached the house, "Mary was doing what she felt was right."

"I know she was." Her voice was tight, tense.

He held open the door for her and said nothing more as they dumped their boots and hung their jackets on pegs. Inside, he hunted in the refrigerator and came up with some leftovers from the mac and cheese he'd made the boys two nights ago. "This okay?" he asked, showing her.

"Sure."

"Don't sound so dubious. It's not from the box. I make my own from scratch."

Her cheeks pinkened faintly. "Really? I hate the box stuff."

"So do I. Learning to make my own was a matter of self-defense because the twins love it."

He popped the bowl in the microwave, then started a fresh pot of coffee. In a relatively short time they sat across from one another at the table, steaming bowls of mac and cheese and fresh cups of coffee in front of them.

"This *is* delicious," she remarked after she tasted the first bite.

"I use good cheddar to start with. And the sauce is easy to make."

"Well worth any effort. I didn't know this could taste so good."

"I take it you don't cook much."

She shook her head. "I just can't get up the interest. Not just for myself. My days are long, and it's a lot easier to pop into some place for a little sushi, or a salad."

"I love a good salad," he remarked, "but if that's mostly what you're eating… Are you a health-food nut?"

"I guess I am in some ways. I like my vegetables fresh, I don't usually eat things like bacon, I prefer fish over meat…"

He shook his head. "All you'll get here is down-home cooking."

"Well, you work hard. Until lately, I always spent too much time in a chair."

"Maybe so."

He ate another few mouthfuls, then put his fork down and wiped his mouth with a paper napkin. "Courtney."

"Yes?" She looked up.

"I've been round and round about this, and maybe you need to hear some of it so you can feel easier in your heart."

"Me?" Her eyes widened.

"Yes, you." He hesitated, knowing he was about to rewalk painful territory, but feeling pushed somehow to share these things with her. Mary's death had left a lot of holes in his life, in the boys' lives, in the lives of her friends. And this was one of her friends.

"I married Mary knowing she was in the Guard. She was proud of what she did and I would never have asked her to quit. It was a weekend a month and it seemed to revitalize her in some way. Especially after we married and she worked less at the hospital. She *needed* it. Then the wars started. I could see the handwriting on the wall. I think she could, too. She'd signed on for another six-year commitment. No way out, but I know, I absolutely know, that even if she could have resigned, she would have refused to even consider it. Those troops were *her* troops. And when they got called to active duty, nothing on earth would have stopped her from going with them."

Courtney nodded, compressing her lips as if she were holding back powerful feelings.

"She knew it would be a hardship for me and the boys. But she couldn't resist her calling, Courtney. Her sense of duty. She saw this as her *mission.* And if I had even tried to argue against her leaving the boys, I know I'd have heard about all the other families making similar sacrifices. And she would have been right." He sighed. "Believe me, I found this a whole lot harder to accept after she died, and I sometimes still get a bit angry. But in the end I kept coming back to the same place."

Courtney nodded stiffly.

"She felt her medical skills were needed more there than here. I'm sure they were. And I'm as sure as I'm sitting here right now that if I had found a way to prevent her from going, if I had even tried, I would have broken our relationship. I might have even broken something in her."

He waited, noting that Courtney's eyes looked wet, but she said nothing. He plunged on, ignoring the tightness in his own chest.

"So when you feel guilty for asking her to put her ear to the ground with those Iraqi women, I know exactly how she responded. And if you'd warned her a million times that she might get hurt, she would have done it anyway. Neither of you could possibly know what was going to happen. No way did you ask her to do this thinking she'd die. No way. But even if she had suspected she might, she still would have done it. Because that was Mary."

A tear hovered on Courtney's eyelashes, but didn't fall. Dom felt his own eyes burn, but the pain was no longer what it had been two years ago. It had transmuted somehow: still strong, still hard, but it was now something quieter in a way he couldn't quite explain. As if he and grief had settled their fight and become friends of a sort.

"You're right," Courtney said finally. "Even if she had known the eventual outcome, she would have done it."

"Of course she would have. That woman was born to take care of people. To help in any way she could, to fight for those who needed a champion. Sometimes it hurts to admit, but some of the very things I loved most about her were the things that took her away from us."

"You've made peace," she remarked, her voice a little thick.

"Yes, I suppose I have, mostly." He hesitated. "Courtney, you need to make peace, too. You can't be sure she was murdered, no matter how it looks. What will you do if you find out there isn't a bad guy?"

"I don't have enough to put together a case against anyone in particular yet, but I got an email yesterday that removed any doubt that someone on our side was involved."

He stiffened. Anger started a slow creep along his nerve endings. "What did it say?"

"It said they were watching me, that they knew what I was up to."

He swore and jumped to his feet. "And you brought their attention *here?*"

She jumped up, too. "They don't know where I am. There's no way they could know."

"That's not what I hear about the government."

"You're talking *to* the government. There's no way they could follow me. It would cost too damn much and nobody would authorize it. God, Dom, I even removed the battery from my cell phone when I left Georgia. No one followed me. Give me some credit. I know all the ways people can cover their tracks, and all the ways they can be found. I'm smart enough not to leave a trail. If they want to get to me in some way, they'll do it when I go back."

"Maybe." He sighed, letting go of his anger. "Maybe," he said again. "Could you find out who sent the email?"

"No. They used an anonymous server in Finland. No way I can crack it, least of all from here. But what they *did* do was confirm my suspicions. Somebody's up to no good, and they can't be allowed to get away with it."

Looking at her, he could see her near-desperation to settle this. He recognized it because for a long time he'd lived with the same feeling. How do you pick up and carry on when the one you loved was killed? How did you deal with surviving?

It struck him then that survivor guilt was probably part of what was driving her. If she admitted to a sneaking, snaky feeling that she should have been killed in Mary's place, it wouldn't have surprised him.

That thought crumbled some of his resistance to what she was doing. Not all of it, but some of it. He at least had found some kind of resolution within himself. This woman was living with questions that she had to answer somehow.

"Courtney," he said quietly.

She lifted her head again and he saw the sparkle of tears on her lashes. "I'm sorry," she said. "I'll pack and go. I'm sure they don't know where I am, but I can't take the risk. It was wrong of me to come."

"Seems like you didn't really have a choice." His voice was almost gruff, and those tears of hers, even not fully shed, were tearing at him. He felt such sympathy for her and he knew only one response.

He reached out and hugged her. After the barest instant of hesitation, she let herself lean into his embrace, let him stroke her back almost awkwardly.

"Don't feel guilty," he murmured. "Do you really think any of us has control over these things, over who lives and who dies? If you're right, these guys got Mary. Given a chance, they'd have probably gotten you, too. If there's one thing I've learned to live with, it's that it's all luck of the draw."

He felt her head tip, so he pulled back just a hair so they could look at each other's faces.

"Luck of the draw?" she repeated. "Some luck."

"Surely you've seen enough by now to know that's all it is. I know it's hard to live with. We all like to control things as much as we can. But when you come down to it, we really don't control anything at all."

"Maybe." She blinked and one tear ran down her face.

He lifted a finger to wipe it away. Her blue eyes darkened at the touch and he felt his own body leap in response. Heat exploded in him as if someone had ignited gunpowder.

God, he wanted her. And he didn't want to want her.

She must have read something in his face, because all of a sudden she pulled back, away, out of his arms.

Feeling a burst of self-disgust, he dropped back into his chair. What was happening to him? Couldn't he restrain his randy impulses? Had it been so long that he'd forgotten how?

"Maybe," she said, "I should just go upstairs."

He knew what she meant, and more than anything he didn't want her to feel she needed to run from him. It had just been a moment, after all.

"If you like," he said, making his tone indifferent. "Or we can talk some more and you can eat more than a sparrow."

She hesitated, then slowly sank back on the chair. Her tears were gone, and she regarded him as if he had just grown two heads. And maybe he had.

He cleared his throat. "What made you decide to join NCIS?"

"What made you decide to become a rancher?" she countered.

At least he could manage a smile. "I never wanted to be anything else. Dad sent me away to college so I could experience other stuff, but I just wanted to get back here. Those four years seemed like an eternity. Now you."

"I grew up wanting to get into law enforcement. My dad was a cop. He died in the line of duty, and they never found his killer."

"What happened?"

"An all-too-common story. Nighttime traffic stop on a deserted road. Back then they didn't have dashboard cameras, and nobody ever saw who he pulled over. He radioed in a license plate number, but it turned out to belong to a car stolen in another state, a car they never located. They found Dad over an hour later, after he failed to make radio contact again."

"I'm sorry."

"Yeah. Me, too. I wanted to be a cop before that, but after that I wanted to be something more. An investigator."

He nodded, understanding. "And that's why you're so fired up to get justice for Mary."

"Maybe." She looked down at her plate, picked up her fork and pushed cheesy macaroni around in a random pattern. "Yes, probably so. I can't even find words to tell you how much justice means to me."

"You want to see them in prison?"

"It's not that. I want *answers*. It's so hard for a family not to know, not to see someone at least accused. To not know that someone cares enough to try to get the perp. I can live with it when I build a case but the accused gets acquitted. It happens, it's awful, but it happens. And when it happens, it probably means I was wrong, or I didn't do enough. It burns in my gut, but at least I know we tried. What I can't stand is not trying. Throwing up your hands and saying, 'We'll never know.' I can't stomach that."

Dom turned that around in his head, thinking it over. "So if you finish here, and find nothing, will you be able to let it rest?"

"Once I've turned over every single stone and shovelful of manure, yes. But only then. For now I don't know enough. But I sure as hell know we haven't done anywhere near enough to get this guy or these guys. That's intolerable."

He nodded. "I can respect that."

Her gaze leaped to his. "So you don't hate me for this?"

"The thought never crossed my mind."

"But you were angry."

"Of course I was angry. I'd put it all to bed mostly, then all of a sudden somebody was standing there telling me we were going to rake it all up again. That maybe I didn't even know the truth about what happened. Of course I got mad. I didn't want to walk through that valley again."

"I'm sorry."

He shook his head. "The thing is, it's doing me some good."

"How so?"

"I'm realizing that while I get a little mad about it, about stirring it up again, I'm not falling into the pit this time. I'm actually mostly on an even keel. That would make Mary happy, I think."

"I'm sure it would. She was generous to her soul."

"Yeah." He nodded, and was surprised to feel himself smiling at the memory. "She made me promise that if anything happened to her, I'd get on with life. And I've been feeling a bit guilty lately because I've basically been living frozen in time. Keeping too busy to think, looking after the boys and the ranch, but little else. I'm sure if she'd been around, she'd have given me hell about it."

"I can almost hear her doing that."

"So maybe," he said quietly, "we'll both find a little rest with this over the next few days."

"Maybe," she agreed. "I know that's what I came here for."

Chapter 5

Dom found Courtney easy to teach. She seemed to have an intuitive understanding of what he was trying to accomplish with his horses, and she followed directions perfectly. He kept a lead rein on the horse as they practiced in the arena, but she didn't really need it.

She got the part about dropping the bit to one side, rather than pulling on the reins after just three tries. She learned how to lean in the saddle to let the horse know what she wanted in surprisingly short order.

"You're one of the best trainees I've ever had," he told her as she reached a nice trot, relaxed in the saddle and smiled.

"Well," she said on a laugh, "I know how *I'd* want to be treated."

"That's it in a nutshell," he agreed. "A light hand, a gentle touch. That's all they need."

He asked her to stop, and was pleased with the way she shifted her weight and pushed into the stirrups. The horse,

Marti, who'd liked her so much at their first meeting, obeyed immediately. Of course, he'd chosen Marti for this exercise because she was gentle and obliging by nature. She had been the first mount for his boys as well, and had tolerated their youthful mistakes almost as if they were her own colts.

"I'm going to take the lead off now," he said. "You'll be on your own."

"Really?" She looked both excited and a little frightened, but as soon as he unsnapped the lead she leaned forward in the saddle, patted Marti's neck, and said, "Let's see what we can do, you lovely lady."

Marti tossed her head and snorted in a way that for her always meant she was pleased. Well, of course she was pleased. Her rider was proving adept, and Marti had never really liked the lead. She tolerated it, almost as if she understood its necessity at times, but it was obvious from her posture and her eyes that she vastly preferred to be guided by her rider.

That spark was there now, a horse's way of smiling, as Marti's step took on a bit of a prance, hooves lifting just a little higher.

"Now just pay attention to Marti," he advised her. "She'll take care of you if you mess up. She's very smart."

"Oh, I can tell she's smart already."

He now saw the spark in Courtney, too, a lightening in her face that made her lovely. He felt a pang for love lost, and a pang that he was apparently emerging from the frigid wasteland of grief enough to notice another woman. It would be easy to feel guilty about that.

But as his pastor had said to him once, "Mary wouldn't want you to commit suttee."

Yet it was hard not to feel guilty when you still had a life and someone you loved did not. Hard to feel an awakening from the winter of grief.

He knew what Mary would have wanted for him. That knowing didn't make it one damn bit easier.

After her riding lesson, Courtney got her first lessons in grooming. She enjoyed running the brush over Marti, and loved the way Marti appeared to enjoy the attention. In a matter of a few hours, she began to understand why Dom loved this life so much. It would be easy, she thought, to fall in love with the rhythm of the days, the work, the horses. Her muscles, accustomed to workouts in gyms and jogging, actually liked this different kind of exercise and, without question, it was much more emotionally satisfying.

Afterward, she took the hot bath Dom recommended, luxuriating in the relaxing hot water until it started to become tepid. She cleaned the tub, checked to make sure she had left everything as spotless as she had found it, then dressed and headed downstairs again.

The file box still awaited her. The tapes she had not yet been able to make herself listen to. The envelopes full of photos from Iraq that she had barely opened.

And the sight of them reminded her of yesterday's email.

Her heart accelerated a little, and once again she went over all the measures she'd taken to cover her real destination and her real purpose in this "vacation." Could somebody have really found out where she was?

Of course. So the question became was she putting Dom and his boys at risk? Very unlikely. Clearly if he'd known anything, Dom would have raised a ruckus long ago. So she didn't have to worry that she was putting them at risk. Conviction filled her. Yes, they would be safe. If anyone was a risk, it was her, and she was fairly good at taking care of herself.

Besides, even if someone found she was here, why would

they care? She had been Mary's friend, and it wasn't out of line for her to visit Mary's family.

Unease wouldn't quite leave her, though. Getting an email like that would make anyone uneasy. All that mattered anyway, was that she was certain Dom and his boys were at no risk at all. For herself...well, sometimes she just didn't care.

It was hard to care quite so much about living when you sometimes felt that you should have been the one killed.

God, she felt more reluctance to go into that box than she would have ever believed possible. Her instincts had driven her to come here in defiance of her orders, but never had she imagined just how painful it would become to have to see those photos and listen to Mary's voice again.

She gave herself a mental shake, trying to shed the personal feelings and focus herself intellectually. She was an investigator. This was just another investigation. Regardless of her history with Mary, it was essential she put her feelings on hold.

With another cup of coffee, she headed back into the office and opened the box. She couldn't afford to let her heart break. Not now.

Nor did it help that the more time she spent with Dom, the more attractive she found him. As she sat and lifted the box lid to reveal the stack of emails, tapes and photos, she caught herself whispering, "I'm sorry, Mary. I hope you don't mind."

But even as she whispered the words, she knew it wasn't Mary who would mind; it was herself.

Shaking her head, she dived into the box, facing the pain because someone *had* to make every attempt to find Mary's killer. To find those men who had terrorized the Iraqi women. All of them deserved justice, and she was the last stop on that train.

* * *

A few hours later, she rubbed her eyes and then stretched, looking up from her work. Nothing so far had seemed unusual or out-of-the-way. Most of Mary's snapshots seemed to be of her coworkers and the town where she had run her ad hoc clinic for local women. No pictures of her patients, of course. But photos of them wouldn't have helped anyway.

And she still hadn't gotten to the audiotapes, or the CDs. Mary evidently hadn't missed sending something nearly every single day.

Picking up her mug, she went to the kitchen where she could hear Dom talking to the boys, who had come home from school just a little while ago. They were at the table with their homework and snacks and Dom was sitting with them.

"Coffee's fresh," he said when he saw her.

"Thanks, I need it."

Kyle piped up, "You're coming camping with us. That's awesome."

She had to smile. "Awesome indeed," she agreed. "I'm looking forward to it."

"I can hardly wait," Todd announced. "I want to go now."

"Nope," Dom said firmly. "You haven't finished your homework, we still need to pack and then it'll be too late to go today."

Todd scowled. "I hate homework."

"What would you rather do?"

"Ride!"

Kyle looked at his brother. "I *like* homework."

"Do not."

"Do, too!"

"Okay," Dom said quietly, and the argument ended right there. The boys exchanged scowls, but returned to their books and papers.

Dom gave Courtney a crooked look of amusement. She flashed him a smile and continued her trip to the coffeepot.

"Anything?" he asked her.

She shook her head.

"I didn't think so." Then he returned his attention to his sons.

She paused after she rinsed her mug and gazed at the three dark heads at the table. Something about the grouping tightened her throat. Loneliness, she supposed. Oh, she had plenty of friends, but this was a different kind of togetherness, the kind she hadn't known since her mother had died a few years ago. Family.

She had always assumed in a vague way that someday she'd have a family of her own. It had always been out there somewhere on her horizon, an inchoate vision of that family and future. But now she was just past thirty, and that vision was beginning to dim. As she stood there, she realized she had begun to plan a solitary future, as if something inside her told her that family was never meant to be hers, or that the opportunity had somehow passed her by.

Which was ridiculous. Thirty-year-old women were hardly over-the-hill these days. Unfortunately, reason and emotion could be miles apart, and right now emotion told her she'd never know the moments Dom enjoyed at this instant with his sons.

She smothered a sigh, told herself not to sink into a pit of ridiculous self-pity, and refilled her mug.

"Going back to work?" Dom asked as she turned away from the pot.

"I was. Do I need to be doing something else?"

"Not yet. Later I'll need to pack the clothes you want to bring, but for now the only people who need to do something are two boys who are dawdling."

"We're not," came two voices in unison.

Dom glanced at them.

Pack her stuff? Courtney paused, then gave a laugh.

"What?" Dom asked.

"Of course I can't carry my clothes in a suitcase on horseback. Duh."

That sent the boys off into peals of laughter, and the corners of Dom's mouth twitched as his eyes twinkled. "The horses hate suitcases."

"I can't imagine why," she said drily.

"Because they bang around!" Todd supplied.

"I think," Dom said, "that Ms. Courtney already figured that out."

"Oh."

Dom looked at Courtney, indicating his sons with a jerk of his head. "Too young yet for sarcasm."

"What's that?" Kyle demanded.

"Trust me, you'll figure it out in the next few years. In fact, I'm sure you'll be full of it."

Courtney laughed again. "I seem to remember becoming full of it around ten."

"Sounds about right to me."

She wanted to linger with them, but decided she was probably impeding the homework, so she gave them a smile and returned to the office. And returned to the godawful job of pawing through the bones of a love she wished she could find.

Just as she was finally getting to the bottom of the stack of photos, with darkness creeping in and the smells of dinner cooking, she came across a photograph that made her pause.

There was nothing about it specifically. Or maybe there was. She turned on another light, and peered at the image, trying to figure out what bothered her.

It was a photo taken in the Iraqi town. Courtney even

recognized it as being taken from the door of the clinic Mary had established, looking across the street at a small shop. Women in long, dark dresses, many with their faces covered as well as their hair, were walking by. Some of the shops wares were on creaky folding tables out front, and one woman had paused to look. A couple of soldiers were in the photo, too.

One had his back to the camera and seemed to be involved in a conversation with a smiling Iraqi man. The other faced toward the camera, and she thought she recognized him. Well, she recognized a lot of soldiers who were stationed in that part of Iraq, mainly because her job required her to be there so often.

But this one...something niggled at her. She glanced at the date on the photo and saw that it was just a few days before Mary had been killed.

She looked at the soldier's face again, and wished it were larger.

She jumped up from the desk, driven by an instinct from years of this kind of work. It might be wrong, but something told her she needed a closer look at that soldier's face.

"Dom?" She burst into the kitchen and found him standing at the stove, stirring a pot. The boys had vanished somewhere.

"Yeah?" He looked over his shoulder.

"Do you have a magnifying glass? A scanner?"

"I have both." He glanced at the photo she held. "Did you find something?"

"I don't know. But something in this photo caught my attention. I need a better look at it."

"Just a second."

He turned down the heat beneath the pot, stirred it a couple of more times, then turned to her.

"That smells good," she said.

"Beef stew. Hearty and filling. Probably not up your alley."

She flushed faintly. "Actually, it smells like it's right up my alley."

A nearly silent laugh escaped him. "Okay, let's go magnify this photo."

In the office he pulled out a good-size rectangular magnifying glass and turned on some more lights. He waited patiently while she pored over the photo.

Something in that guy's expression seriously disturbed her, but the magnifying glass wasn't enough. She looked up. "Scanner?"

"Right here." He touched a button on his computer and it sprang out of hibernation quickly. Then he took the photo from her and placed it on a flatbed scanner. Bending over, he pressed the button on the scanner, then typed something into his computer.

"Okay," he said, "it'll come up as a file on the desktop labeled Iraq-one. You probably know what to do from there. I have to get back to dinner before I scorch it."

Since he had turned the heat down on the stew, she suspected it was more of a matter of not wanting to see the photo enlarged, or discover what it was she didn't like.

"Thank you," she said as he left the room. Then she took his chair at his desk and waited for the scan to finish.

When it was done, she opened the file and worked on cutting that man's face out of the photo and enlarging it in stages. Some of the resolution was lost, of course, but as she fiddled with size and other settings, at last his expression leaped out at her. And what had bothered her became obvious.

He was staring right at Mary. And the look on his face was enough to make her shiver. Even so, she had seen that expression on the face of other soldiers who'd been through a lot of combat. What disturbed her even more was the sense that she should know that guy.

She hesitated only a few moments before she set his face as a separate file. Then she emailed it to one of her best friends in the service, Lena Mattock.

She asked for a face-recognition match, and a background on the guy if they identified him. She said nothing about why, and hoped there was nothing left in the in the picture to give away where the photo had been taken, other than somewhere sunny. She checked one last time before sending, to be sure. No, no one should be able to tell where the photo had been taken.

She didn't doubt Lena would run the face through the software. Lena was the kind of person who would just assume Courtney had some valid reason, and wouldn't bother to ask why.

And maybe, finally, she'd learn something useful.

Chapter 6

"Were you an only child?" Courtney asked as she watched Dom pack the requisite clothes in large saddlebags.

"Yeah. Mom almost died having me, so Dad wouldn't hear of letting her try again."

"Any other family?"

"I have an uncle in New York." Dom flashed a smile. "The city lights attracted him more than dark starry nights. I see him and his family every now and then, but none of them seems too keen on roughing it out here, and I can't leave for long to visit them."

Courtney nodded. "I was an only, too. I don't really know if that was a choice, or if it just happened that way. My parents never talked about it, one way or the other."

"I know you said your dad passed, but what about your mom?"

"She lives in Taos now. She moved there for the artistic community."

"What does she do?"

"She's a potter. Good enough to support herself."

Dom's eyes crinkled at the corners. "You must seem almost alien to her."

Courtney chuckled. "Sometimes I think so. She never wanted me to go into law enforcement and keeps telling me I need to loosen up. Maybe she's right."

"We are who we are." Dom shrugged and folded some more clothing into a saddlebag.

Much truth in that, Courtney thought. "Those saddlebags look like they've seen a lot."

"They're pretty old all right. Sometimes I have to get them restitched, but the leather never comes close to wearing out as long as I take care of it."

"How long will the ride be tomorrow?"

He cocked an eyebrow at her. "Worrying about saddle sores?"

"Only a little."

"It's a couple of hours, actually, but we can walk some of it to give you and the horses a break. It's not like we'll need a lot of time for gathering the herd. The dogs'll do most of the work getting them into the pen, and then in the morning we'll move 'em down here."

"Those dogs are pretty amazing."

"They are." He stuffed the last of her clothes into a second saddlebag, then started adding her personal care items, along with a towel and washcloth. "I'm thinking about getting a new one this fall."

"How come?"

"Bradley is getting up there. He's almost ten. I think he's going to start looking for a warm place by the fire soon."

"Won't that add a lot to your work, training a dog, too?"

He laughed. "These dogs are born with the instinct to herd. The other dogs do most of the teaching."

"Really?" That surprised her.

"Really. They're social critters, and they want to please. A youngster will know instinctively about herding, and the older dogs will show him when and how. And probably nip him gently when he gets too rambunctious. It's always fun to watch."

"I'd love to see that."

"Well, it won't be for a few weeks yet."

The implication being that she would be long gone by then. And of course she would. She had a job to get back to, and he probably didn't want her to hang around any longer than necessary.

What truly surprised her was that she felt an unexpected reluctance to leave. Good heavens, she'd only been here two days and she was already getting attached? Not good.

Dom finished the packing then suggested they have some coffee in the living room. A courteous host, she told herself, not an indicator that he wanted to spend more time with her. But the boys had gone to bed a half hour ago and the night was still young, even with the early rising he planned.

So she agreed, because there was nothing else she could do. She couldn't bear looking through more photos, or listening to those tapes. There had been enough of that today. The only other alternative was taking a chilly walk, but her leg muscles were beginning to notice her riding lesson, if only mildly. Nor did she want to go sit upstairs in the solitude of the guest bedroom.

All good reasons to justify doing what she really wanted to do: be with Dom.

Something about his quiet steadiness drew her, apart from the fact that he was an awfully attractive man. She liked the sense that he had found balance in his life, something she still sought for herself. She was apt to go overboard on things, most especially her work. Like a dog with a bone, once she took on something, she'd gnaw on it until she'd gnawed it to nothing.

Dom, on the other hand, seemed better able to let things take their own course in their own way. But, of course, she didn't know him all that well yet. She probably never would.

"Something wrong?" he asked as they settled in the living room.

"Not really." She was hardly going to tell him what she was thinking about. So she covered. "Just feeling kind of wistful, I guess."

"Eager to get back to…where *are* you stationed now?"

"Not especially eager to get back, no. I was at Camp Lejeune for over a year. We had a really full investigation load, mainly because we covered two states and an awful lot of sailors and marines and their families. But about eight months ago I got assigned to Georgia, to the Contingency Response Field Office." She paused. "I guess that's because of the training I had before I got sent to the Middle East."

"Meaning?"

"Well, we're kind of a SWAT team, of sorts. Counterintelligence, counterterrorism, force protection, all the high-risk stuff. We're a rapid deployment group, ready to go anywhere we're needed, fast, in support of other NCIS field offices."

He studied her a moment and said, "Why do I think you're not very happy about that?"

She gave a humorless laugh. "I'm an investigator. I don't get to do much investigating at the moment. No, now I'm training all the time to be the best of the best or something like that. The military-type training is something I never really wanted. I just wanted to be an investigator. But I suppose they're teaching me to be a better one. At the very least I'm learning to slot in quickly with different teams and their investigations, learning to arrive in the middle of something that's ongoing and so awful that it can't wait indefinitely for resolution."

"But it's not something you volunteered for?"

"No. You don't get to volunteer all the time. I was selected. I could have refused it but…"

"But what?" he prodded gently when she fell silent.

"Frankly? I was chafing at Lejeune. I think I know why they pulled me out of the Middle East and sent me there. It was so I couldn't make any more noise about Mary. They hoped I'd get so busy so fast I wouldn't have time to think about her. It almost worked. But maybe somebody sensed that I was still nosing around a bit."

"Were you?"

"Most definitely. So off to CRFO, where I don't have the tools to pursue a cold case. Where if I even tried I'd probably get disciplined, because that's not my mission now by any stretch of the imagination. No, my job now is to prepare for upcoming problems, to be ready to go tactical at a moment's notice, to join other teams in a crisis, basically."

"That sounds elite."

"That's a matter of perception I suppose."

He hesitated, reaching for his coffee cup, and sipping before he spoke. "Do you really think they're trying to shut you down?"

She didn't answer immediately. The truth was, when looking at it in those terms, she couldn't say that. Not honestly. Not even after the email. That had come from a person, not the NCIS. "Truthfully? No. I don't think there's some grand conspiracy to keep me from finding out who killed Mary, or who those rapists are."

"Then what *do* you think, really?"

"That the NCIS doesn't care beyond what they consider to be a rational allocation of resources. That overall they judged this situation to be wasting those resources in terms of continued investigation. Because, honestly, we didn't come up with anything useful in a couple of weeks, and if you don't find anything useful by then, especially in a war zone where evidence can't be protected and people won't talk, the likelihood we'd get a bead on Mary's killer was slim at best. Especially when it had a lot of the aspects of an insurgent attack."

He nodded.

"So basically, while there might be an individual or two who have something of a *real* reason for wanting me to leave desert ghosts alone, the organization as a whole doesn't care except that I not waste their time and money on a case there's almost no hope of resolving."

"So maybe they sent you to CRFO—did I get that right?— simply to put you to best use. Maybe they figure you're flexible and smart enough to do a tough job."

"Maybe. That's what I'd like to believe."

"But you don't."

She sighed and shook her head. "I'm not paranoid by nature, Dom, but something about this stinks somehow. It stinks to high heaven. Sometimes I wonder if they're trying to protect me by yanking me away from this case, rather than just shut me up."

He stiffened a little. "You think Mary's killer could come after *you?*"

"That sounds paranoid to the extreme, doesn't it? I don't know. That's the problem in a nutshell, I don't know. I have instincts. Intuitions. They tell me something is going on. But just what's going on I don't know."

He fell silent, sipping coffee, clearly ruminating. After a minute or so he remarked, "So I need to keep an eye on you."

"On me? Why?"

"I wouldn't want anything to happen to you while you're here."

"I told you, no one knows where I am. I didn't tell a soul. And even if I had, I only expected to stay a few hours."

He nodded slowly.

Uneasiness began to prickle along her nerves. "Dom, no one knows where I am but you. Even so, like I said, I have no reason to think someone would come after me personally, except maybe to fire me."

"And you're probably right."

"Of course I am. If I had any reason to think otherwise, I wouldn't have brought trouble with me to the door of Mary's husband and kids."

One side of his mouth curved upward. "I don't think you would have. But I don't stay in business by ignoring even the remotest possibilities that occur to me."

"Well," she said, putting her mug down, "if you think it's even a remote possibility, then I should leave now." The second time that day she had tried to leave. This time it occurred to her that she might not be trying to escape his suspicions, that she might have brought a threat to his door. Why? Because she didn't believe anyone would have bothered to follow her. If they wanted her out of the way, there were ample opportunities during her training in Georgia.

No, she was trying to escape her growing attraction to Dom, and the discomfort that came with it. *Chicken.*

She rose, but he rose instantly and reached out, taking her upper arm in a gentle grip. "No. You're not leaving." He released her quickly. "We're going camping with the boys this weekend. They're looking forward to it. Frankly, so am I."

She watched as his gaze drifted down to her mouth, then lower to the mounds of her breasts. In an instant his eyes snapped away, but she had caught the look, and her entire body responded to it in a flash.

No, she told herself. No. But it had happened, and she couldn't deny that it had. Standing there, looking at Dom as he turned back to his chair, she knew she was getting into deep trouble. Their worlds intersected at only one point: Mary. That wasn't enough to build on. In fact, it was a damn good reason to keep clear.

Slowly she sank back onto the couch, hoping her cheeks didn't look as flushed as they felt. She had come here hoping to find a clue to a killer, not a romance, not a passion, not a fling. Nothing was going to change that, not her unexpectedly strong response to him, nor even the way her arm tingled where he had touched her.

She leaned back in the couch and lifted her mug again for something to do with her hands. Because, disturbingly enough, they itched to touch Dom. To find out if those wiry muscles were as hard as they looked. To trace the contours of his face and discover if his lips were hard or soft, to put her hands on his narrow hips and…

Whoa! She looked down into her coffee as she waited for her suddenly racing heart to slow down. Wrong time, wrong place, wrong guy.

Too bad her body wouldn't listen.

She tried to tell herself she was feeling an attraction to an American archetype: the good-looking cowboy. Unfortunately, she already knew it was more than that. His gentleness, his inner quietude and calm…those seemed far more attractive to her than just his rugged face or well-built body.

She could easily understand why Mary had fallen in love with him. He must have seemed like an oasis of peace to a woman who daily dealt with health emergencies and high stress.

"So you're SWAT now?" Dom asked, apparently feeling a desire to fill the silence.

"I'm training, yes. I most likely won't be used in that

capacity, even if there's a call for it. But we all get the same training."

He shook his head. "That's some job."

"It can be an adrenaline rush at times." She shifted a bit uneasily on the couch. "I'm not really an adrenaline junkie. It's not something I need or want. Sometimes it comes with the job, or life events, but it's just not my thing."

"Mary was an adrenaline junkie." He said it without any hint of judgment.

"Yes, she was. Not that she went out looking for things to give her that rush, but she certainly seemed more comfortable with it than I am."

"No, let's be honest here." Dom sighed. "Mary needed it. Not in a bad way, but she thrived on it. Which is why she worked in an emergency room, and why being in Iraq never overwhelmed her. It might wear her out, but it lifted her, too. I'm not saying there's anything wrong with that. We need people who can thrive in those circumstances."

"We do," she agreed. "What about you?" She asked even though she already suspected the answer.

"I deal with it, but I'd rather avoid it if possible. I prefer an even flow to my days. You could say I'm a river and Mary was a waterfall."

The comparison drew a smile out of Courtney. "That's apt. For Mary at least." And she liked the idea of Dom as a slow-moving river, steady and reliable.

"I never could figure what she saw in me," he admitted. "I'm dull by comparison."

She shook her head instantly, troubled that he felt that way. "You know, waterfalls need rivers. Rivers feed them."

At that he gave a quick laugh. "Maybe so. Maybe so."

No maybe about it, Courtney thought. She suspected that Dom's steadiness was the river from which Mary drew some of her strength. And she could certainly see why.

All of a sudden a knock came from the front door. Dom looked a little puzzled as he rose and went to answer it. Opening it, he revealed a large man in a deputy's uniform.

"Micah," he said, sounding surprised.

"You hole up any more, man, and we'll send out search parties."

Courtney watched as he invited the tall, exotic-looking man inside.

"Courtney, this is Micah Parish, an old friend. Micah, Courtney Tyson. You two might have a bit in common. Courtney's with NCIS. Coffee?"

"You know I never turn down coffee." Micah crossed the living room in a couple of strides, and offered his hand to Courtney. "My pleasure. So I take it you're not here on a social visit?"

Courtney hesitated, and Dom came to her rescue. "Well, she will be over the weekend, when she goes camping with us."

Micah evidently was too sharp to let it pass. "I see. Or do I?"

Dom hesitated, then said as he turned toward the kitchen, "She thinks Mary was murdered."

Dom continued on his way to get the coffee, but Micah almost visibly stiffened. His pitch-black gaze sharpened as he looked at Courtney. "You sure about that?" he asked.

"Not enough to charge anyone yet."

"But you can't live with not knowing?"

"No," Courtney admitted. "No. I can't."

Micah nodded slowly, then folded himself onto the other easy chair, the one Dom didn't use. As if he were very familiar with this house and its customs.

"Fragging, we used to call it," he said, his gaze still fixed to her. "Now why would someone want to frag Mary? She was a good woman."

"She was my informant on a case involving the rape of some Iraqi women most likely by a couple of our marines."

"That would do it, all right."

Dom returned carrying a mug for Micah and topped off all the cups before he returned the pot to the kitchen. Micah lifted his and took a deep swallow, waiting, as if he didn't want to discuss anything until Dom was present.

"So what got you all riled up enough to come out here?" Dom asked as he resumed his seat.

Micah's head tilted a bit. "Maude mentioned you and the boys didn't come in for dinner tonight."

"Who's Maude?" Courtney asked.

"She owns the diner in town," Dom replied. "I didn't suggest we go tonight because you're not all that fond of fatty foods."

"And Maude," Micah remarked patting his flat stomach, "sure knows how to pile on the fat."

"Oh. Well, you should have gone anyway," Courtney said. "I can manage."

"That would be rude," Dom said.

But Courtney was still thinking about something else. "So you and the boys skip a meal at a diner and someone notices?"

"Small town," Micah said. "Everyone notices just about everything. Maude was naturally worried, but for Maude alone I wouldn't have got worried enough to barge in. No, you missed your usual feed run on Thursday, and Cal Barkel mentioned it."

Courtney felt an urge to laugh. "So around here you'd better keep to your usual schedule?"

"So it seems," Micah remarked. His dark eyes danced a bit.

Dom shook his head. "I don't need to make a feed run until sometime next week. As you can see, we're alive and well."

Micah nodded again, sipped his coffee. "Ms. Tyson's arrival must have hit you like a ton of bricks."

"Yes. Briefly. In the end, though, it doesn't make a whole lot of difference to us."

"It could wind up making a big difference psychologically."

Courtney flushed. For the first time it occurred to her there might have been other reasons for telling her to let desert ghosts lie. Reasons that had nothing to do with justice but rather with the feelings of the family. It was entirely possible that her thirst for justice and knowledge wasn't shared by everyone.

But almost immediately her resolve stiffened again. No one could possibly want murderers on the loose. Murderers and rapists. No one.

"I'll be fine, Micah," Dom said. "It won't change my circumstances one bit. And I suspect Mary would want those rapists caught, if Courtney can do it."

"She most definitely wanted them caught," Courtney agreed, feeling a warm flush of gratitude toward Dom. "She wouldn't have agreed to work with me otherwise."

"That's my feeling," Dom said. "It's what Mary would have wanted. For me, it doesn't change one damn thing."

Later, upstairs alone in his bedroom, Dom stared out through a window over his moonlit pastures and outbuildings. He could see the horses, quiet in the night, thinking about whatever things horses thought about on moonlit nights when the world was quiet and no threats stalked them.

He tried to keep his own life as simple as that of his horses, but of course, no human could ever live that simply. And he honestly wasn't sure that horses didn't face their own complexities, both in surviving and caring for their young, and in dealing with humans.

But right now they were relaxed and hardly moving, guarded by three dogs who sometimes probably irritated them, but likely made them feel more secure, too.

Old Native American stories told of how wolves often came into their encampments and spent the night among the horses, without disturbing them, waiting for a chance to pounce on some tossed away food morsel. Maybe horses and wolves had a longer history than most people realized. Like humans and wolves. Certainly his dogs seemed to prefer the company of the horses, although when the winter started to get bitter they often wanted some time in the barn or the house. By contrast, the horses simply hunkered together and shifted positions so that none of them was always on the outside of the herd's gathering, bearing the brunt of the wind.

Wolves, horses and people. They took care of their own kind, and sometimes they took care of each other's kind. The dynamics always fascinated him.

Like Micah coming to check on him tonight because he'd missed his two regular trips to town. Trips he'd started making for the sake of the boys, to give them something to look forward to. Back when they were little and Mary was still with them, those trips had been a lot less frequent. But now…the boys needed them. And maybe he did, too, at least some of the time. Contact with others of his kind.

He hoped Mary approved of how he was handling the boys. But she probably did or she wouldn't have been willing to leave them with him while she went to Iraq. She must have believed he was a good enough dad to be a bit of a mom, too.

He sure hoped so.

Regardless, tonight he was aware of how much he'd sunk into routine. At first it had saved him from anxiety about Mary, and then from grief over her. There was always something that needed doing, something that he could get out of the way rather than put off.

But Courtney's arrival had made him look at himself and his life with fresh eyes. He wondered how dull she found it. Maybe even sad.

He didn't find it dull or sad himself, but he was uneasily aware that not everyone would agree. Maybe not even Mary who had clearly needed more in her life than the ranch.

"I'm sorry," he whispered into the empty darkness. "I'm sorry, Mary."

He guessed he'd been inadequate in some ways, although Mary never once complained. She certainly had known how he lived when she had married him.

He pressed his forehead to the chilly glass of the window, no longer seeing the horses or anything else. He felt as if Mary were standing beside him, as she often had when they'd looked out on their shared world before tumbling into bed.

Courtney. He could only imagine how alien his life must seem to *her*. But not even that could unsettle him as much as the building attraction he felt for her. It was an attraction he didn't want. It could lead to nothing good. He wasn't the kind of man to have flings, and she wasn't the kind of woman who would want to bury herself on a ranch.

But the initial guilt he had felt for noticing Courtney as a woman had faded with surprising speed. No, he didn't feel guilty about it anymore. It wasn't a betrayal of Mary in even the remotest sense to feel the natural attraction of a man for a woman.

And it was just attraction. She'd leave, probably early next week, and it would fade away, lost among many more powerful memories.

She was too thin, he reminded himself. Not his type at all. He was probably just feeling the natural urges of a man who'd been celibate for a few years. Nothing more.

But even to himself that sounded weak. There was something else he liked about Courtney, something that was drawing him besides the sexual. How did he know that?

Because she wasn't his type.

The almost circular reasoning amused him for a moment or two, and he lifted his head from the glass to look out again at his pastures, his horses.

They were his life. Them and the boys.

He sure as hell didn't need any more complications than he already had.

He started to turn from the window to get ready for bed, and for an instant he thought he heard the light bubble of Mary's laugh. Just an instant.

And for an instant he almost felt her warmth. And even more strongly, he suspected that she *would* be laughing at him. Kindly laughing, but laughing nonetheless.

Mary had never been one to accept psychological bull. Nope. She'd gently argue until you could see how you were deluding yourself. And she'd been good at seeing through those delusions.

"Enjoying yourself, are you?" he asked her in the darkness. He got no answer of course, but he didn't need one. She'd be laughing at him, all right.

But he still had to figure out what was going on with him. Bull or not.

And he didn't like the feeling that it wasn't bull at all.

Chapter 7

In the morning, with thin golden light creeping across a chilly world, the four of them set out on horseback, headed toward the mountains. Dom gave a long, piercing whistle, and a minute later three dogs trotted alongside them.

The twins enjoyed high spirits, talking and laughing. Dom led the way, leading their packhorse, Courtney followed, with the boys behind her. Kyle and Todd had been told to keep an eye on her, and Courtney didn't mind even if they seemed to be more involved in their own conversation and teasing.

They soon entered the woods, fallen leaves and pine needles muffling the hoofbeats even more than the grassy ground. The boys seemed to grow quiet, maybe because they were tired of their verbal play, or maybe it was how the woods seemed to close in around them. Evergreens dominated, but here and there were patches of deciduous trees, still feathered with the colors of autumn, mostly brilliant yellows and dull reds.

With their passage from open meadows into thick trees,

the atmosphere changed. Everything changed. The sun poured in beams through holes in the thick boughs, casting rays that revealed openings beyond what seemed like a thick wall of growth, but it no longer warmed them by striking their backs except every now and then.

The breeze that had nipped at them on open ground vanished and the air became perfectly still. For the first time Courtney felt comfortable enough on her mount to look farther ahead than Dom's back and she noticed the trail they followed seemed awfully narrow, especially as they began to climb more steeply.

Inevitably she noticed his narrow hips and the easy way they swayed in the saddle. A pool of heat settled between her legs and she had to drag her eyes away and force herself to notice something else.

"Dom?"

He swiveled in his saddle, looking back her. "Yeah?"

"How are you going to bring the horses back down this trail? Isn't it kind of narrow?"

"It's a game trail," Kyle or Todd—she still couldn't identify their voices every time—said from behind her. "We don't come back down this way."

"Oh."

"It's just a prettier ride," Dom said. "I thought you'd enjoy the scenery."

"I am." All of it, including the cowboy who rode in front of her, surely the best scenery she'd seen in a while. With effort, she corralled her thoughts and tried to damp down the heat that seemed to ratchet up with every movement of the horse beneath her. "It just suddenly occurred to me that it might be difficult to move twenty or so horses this way. If you had a secret for doing it, I wanted to know."

He laughed. "No secret. Just putting some fun in a workday."

"Well, it *is* beautiful."

So was the view she had of his broad shoulders as he swayed ever so gently with his mount's movements. He wore a lined denim jacket that looked as if it had weathered many, many years, and a black cowboy hat. The whole image was so archetypal that she couldn't help smiling at her own response to it.

Until she looked down and remembered that she was wearing someone else's cowboy boots and someone else's jacket. And that the someone else was probably Mary. She didn't dare ask, and he hadn't offered the information.

Or maybe they were someone else's. Regardless, it was clear it hadn't bothered him to offer them, so she shouldn't be bothered by wearing them.

Except there was that old phrase, the one about stepping into someone else's shoes. Maybe that old saw, at some psychological level, was what was bothering her. Especially in light of her attraction to Dom.

Hell, she thought with a quiet sigh, when did life get so damn complicated? Mary's shoes, Mary's husband, Mary's life.

But they weren't Mary's anymore, were they?

And what did it matter if they were? She was only borrowing a pair of boots, a jacket and a hat. *Borrowing.* No way it would ever be more than that.

The very temporariness of what she was doing eased the twinges of guilt.

Borrowing. Yeah, that's all she was doing, and she'd leave everything just the way she found it.

Her mood lightened abruptly and she gave her attention over to the gorgeous autumn woods. Her mount, Marti, seemed to need no guidance at all. She just kept plodding along behind the packhorse, as if she were content to make this gentle climb forever.

After an hour so, just as they reached a clearing, Dom called a halt. Courtney watched him dismount, drop his reins to the ground, and wondered if she should climb down, too. The boys answered indirectly as they jumped off their own horses.

But before she could move, Dom was there at her side. He smiled up at her, his face shadowed from the sun by the brim of his hat. "Maybe you should let me help. You might be surprised."

He took the reins from her hand, dropped them, then reached up, gripping her waist. She lifted her right leg to pull it from the stirrup and that's when she noticed not everything was right. It felt at once leaden and shaky. She tried to swing it over and it didn't come all the way up.

A quiet chuckle escaped Dom, his hands tightened on her waist and he lifted her down. As soon as her boots hit the ground, her legs almost buckled.

"Steady," he said, keeping his grip on her. "You'll be fine in just a minute or two."

"What happened to my legs?"

"Well, different activity. I don't know how much is fatigue, or how much might be nerves that got a little pinched, or blood flow that got interrupted. I'm not a doctor. I just know this often happens the first time after a long ride. Things'll get back to normal in a minute, though. I promise."

The boys, apparently accustomed to riding, had no trouble making the transition. They whipped around the glade like forces of nature that had been pent up too long, and the dogs tore around at their heels. Watching them, electrically aware of Dom's hands on her waist, she started to smile.

"I take it that this break isn't just for me," she said.

"No way. Those kids can't sit still for too long even on the back of a horse."

"I can see that." She rested a hand on his shoulder for

balance, becoming instantly aware of the muscle beneath the denim. For a second, she felt as if everything inside her stopped in a moment of exquisite awareness, but then, looking down in hopes he wouldn't see her warming cheeks, she shook first one leg and then the other, trying to get some strength back.

And there it was, she realized. If she could stand on one leg now, even for just a few seconds, she was okay. Which meant she no longer needed Dom's support. Unfortunately, she didn't want to relinquish it, either. His hands nearly spanned her entire waist, and for the first time she realized she could like that sensation. She'd never noticed it before with any man. But then had any man ever held her in quite this way?

Maybe not. And inevitably she wondered if Dom felt the snap and sparkle around her waist that she was feeling. Of course he didn't. Why would he?

"Okay?" Dom asked.

"I think so."

He let go of her carefully, not so quickly she'd fall if she didn't have command of her legs back, but quickly enough that she felt he didn't want to touch her. That it disturbed him.

And it probably did. She'd seen the flare of attraction on his face, but she supposed it made him no happier than it made her. If they became partners in passion, they'd become partners in guilt, most likely.

"Thanks." She took a step, then another. Still shaky, but she could walk. "I'm okay."

"Thought you would be. Stroll around and loosen up. I'm going to check the horses."

Kyle and Todd had started a game of tag, and dervishes had nothing on them. The dogs, however, settled in the sun on the grass, watching everything as their tongues lolled.

Courtney wandered around the glade, as feeling came back to her bottom and her legs recovered their strength. Meanwhile

Dom checked every hoof on every horse, checked their saddle girths and their saddlebags. He only seemed to need to make a few minor adjustments. Meanwhile, when he wasn't checking them out, the other horses grazed on drying grasses and even a few low bushes.

One thing that penetrated her awareness was how Wyoming was a whole lot drier than Georgia or the Carolinas. The air held no detectable humidity at all, and somehow the feeling invigorated her. She stretched and turned her face up to the sun, and let go.

It didn't matter that she wore borrowed clothing, didn't matter that tomorrow or the next day she'd have to continue her investigation or move on. For a few wonderful, marvelous minutes, she neither looked ahead nor looked behind. All that mattered was the present moment.

Another thing she could get addicted to here: no intrusions. No cell phone, no computer, no files to pore over. Nothing could reach her here and that meant for once in her life she could live in the here and now.

She heard Dom approach her through the drying grass and opened her eyes. "Do you always feel this way?"

"What way?"

"Like there's no tomorrow, no yesterday. Just right now."

"Often enough." A smile creased the corners of his eyes. "I won't tell you reality never intrudes. Of course it does. But when I'm doing something like this, or working with the horses, I can usually let go of just about everything else. Or when I'm playing with the boys."

One of whom was hurtling his way right now from behind. Dom's smile deepened a bit. Without even looking, his arm unexpectedly shot out in a flash, and he caught Kyle around his waist, lifting him right off his feet.

A shrieking giggle escaped Kyle, followed by a protest. "Dad, put me down before Todd catches me."

Courtney laughed as Dom let the boy slip to his feet. "How did you do that?" she asked as Kyle went tearing off.

"Practice."

Before she could say another word, she was nudged between her shoulder blades so hard from behind that she stumbled forward a step. Dom caught her by her forearm.

"What was that?" she demanded and turned to find Marti right there. "She did that?"

"She has certain expectations." Dom shoved a hand into his jacket pocket and came up with a cube of sugar. "She expects a reward when we take a break. Hold out your hand."

"Me?" Courtney looked at Marti. "She has awfully big teeth."

"She's also very gentle. You rode her, so you should reward her. Just hold your hand flat so she can feel the cube with her lips."

Courtney hesitated, but only briefly. She held out the cube on her palm, hand flat, and then giggled a bit as she felt both velvety lips and the tickling prickle of hairs. Marti took the cube as gently as Dom had promised and Courtney felt thrilled.

"Can I give her another?"

"At the next break. Marti develops habits fast. If you give her two now, she'll start expecting two every time, and that's not really good for her. But she'd probably like a pat or two."

That was easy enough. Standing beside the horse, Courtney stroked her neck, and patted gently. Before long, she laid her cheek against the mare's neck, feeling heat and coarse hair, and hearing the horse's strong, steady heartbeat. Closing her eyes, she soaked it in, listening to the boys grow quieter as they wore down a bit.

This, she thought, could definitely become addictive.

A short while later, they mounted up again and resumed

their climb along the narrow trail. Every so often, another surprise greeted her: a gorgeous ravine, a sparkling waterfall, a copse of brilliantly colored trees. Although as they climbed higher, the trees began to grow barer.

When they finally halted at a log cabin, she could smell snow on the breeze that blew down the mountain. The cabin stood on the edge of woods at the bottom of a huge meadow that rose even higher up the mountain. To one side were a shed and a separate lean-to. A distance away, a pen had been built from pine trunks. Everything looked weathered and old, but still sturdy.

She could see horses scattered along the distant upper edge near more trees and, as if they had been anticipating this visit, they began to slowly move down the meadow toward the people. The dogs whined almost impatiently, but Dom told them to "settle" and they did exactly that, though not without an occasional whimper of protest.

Even though the sun was higher now, the air had definitely grown colder. She helped as much as she could with unloading the horses and carrying things into the cabin with the boys, then Dom put their mounts in the pen to graze and drink. The horses from higher in the pasture were still slowly moving their way, pausing to graze, but moving ever closer.

The cabin itself was minimalist to the extreme: a rough-hewn wooden table with four equally rough-looking chairs, a sink with an old-fashioned handle pump for water, four cots already made up. Only two windows let in light, and they needed a cleaning. They looked as old as the cabin.

Dom lit a fire in an old woodstove. It caught quickly, and soon heat was radiating throughout the cabin.

"This is cozy," Courtney said. And very different from anything she'd known in her life. Even with all her travels, even having been to places where people lived very poor lives, she'd never spent any time in a cabin like this. And she liked it.

"It's our old line shack," he said. "We use it and a couple of others a number of times through the summers. Not a lot of extra room, but nobody usually has to spend more than a night or two here. We come up here to check the fence and make sure all the horses are okay."

"Where *is* the fence?"

The boys giggled. "Way out there," Kyle said, waving an arm grandly.

"It's a big ranch," Dom agreed. "I don't fence it all, though. Part of it is unfenced for a migration corridor."

"What's that?"

Todd answered. "It's for moose and elk and other stuff, so they can migrate."

"Wait. Hold it. I'm a city girl here."

Dom spoke. "It's simple, really. A lot of animals, just like birds, have seasonal migrations to follow the best grazing. Fencing in so much land has interrupted that. So a few years back when the idea of opening migration corridors got some attention, we signed on. We don't want nature to lose to fencing."

Courtney viewed him with new admiration, because she didn't have any trouble imagining a lot of valid economic reasons to not want to turn over part of your land to grazing by wild animals. "I want to learn more about that. I think that's fantastic."

Dom shrugged. "Not all my neighbors agree, especially since we got a wolf pack on Thunder Mountain. They're probably out of Yellowstone up north, and apparently some of the wolves followed the moose and elk herds, and set up a territory here."

"Now that's something I've heard about."

"We have some pretty fiery meetings about it from time to time."

"But it doesn't bother you?"

"Oh, it bothers me that I might occasionally lose a youngster, but on the other hand, the wilderness, including wolves, need to be protected, too. In the long run, it's better for us all."

He looked at the boys.

"Okay," he announced, pulling off his leather gloves. "We're ready. But how about some lunch first?"

The boys liked that idea. Smiling at their eagerness, Courtney helped as best she could as Dom unpacked sandwiches and bottled water.

They sat together at the table on wooden chairs that creaked and squeaked, eating off the waxed paper that had wrapped the sandwiches. Thick sandwiches, full of ham and cheese.

"How come," she asked, "you have to pen the horses? Couldn't you just gather them up in the morning? It doesn't seem to take you long."

"I want to check them out before I make them take a long walk. Make sure none of them is injured, they don't have stones caught in their hooves, that kind of thing. And it's easier to check them once they're penned than while they're wandering all over hell and gone."

"And we get to count," Kyle said. "Make sure they're all there."

Dom favored them with a smile. "That's right. And you make sure I don't miss one."

The boys seemed rather proud of that assignment.

"And what else do you do?" she asked them.

"We help gather them," Todd answered. Even though he said it offhandedly, she could tell he was proud of that.

"These two are becoming great wranglers," Dom said. Both boys grinned at that.

"It's fun," Kyle said.

"Anything I can do to help?" She expected to be told to stay out of the way, but she got a surprise.

Kyle and Todd exchanged looks. "Marti," said Kyle, "pretty much knows what to do."

"Yeah." Todd looked at her. "Just don't get in the way of your horse."

Courtney looked from one to the other, then at Dom. "Meaning?"

"Marti's a good cutter and herder. She'll do all the work for you, really. The question is whether you can keep your seat if she suddenly cuts or takes off after a recalcitrant horse."

She blinked. "I didn't think you had any recalcitrant horses."

Dom laughed and the boys joined him. "That depends," he said when his laughter eased. "They have moods, too."

"Then maybe it's best if I keep my feet on the ground."

Then Kyle said something that punctured the mood. "Mom never did this with you, did she, Dad?"

Courtney quickly looked down at the sandwich she would never be able to finish, suddenly wishing she were anywhere else on the planet.

"No," Dom said quietly. "She had a different job, remember?"

"A nurse." Kyle nodded vehemently. "I know. I just think it's neat that Miss Courtney wants to help."

Courtney stole a quick look at Dom, trying to gauge his mood. He seemed fine, although the smile had vanished. "People are different," he said mildly enough.

"I know," Kyle said. For him the subject was over.

But Courtney wasn't sure it was over for Dom. He was quieter through the remainder of lunch and she wondered what memories had just been raked up, and whether they were good ones.

None of her business, she reminded herself. She'd be gone

for good in a couple of days. But she gave herself a mental kick anyway. Not once, absolutely not once, had she even considered the pain she might inflict by coming here.

No, she'd been so fixated on justice, and the assumption that Dom would want answers about Mary every bit as much as she still wanted them about her dad, that she hadn't even thought.

Her chest tightened both with sorrow and self-disgust. Yeah, just head west like some kind of idiot to ask questions. She asked questions all the time as an investigator and she didn't often think about the impact of those questions.

Why would she, since usually she was questioning perps and witnesses? But this was different. If she'd been able to shake her obsession for even ten minutes, she might have realized it.

These people had made peace with the past, with the story they'd been given. So, like some kind of unexpected tornado, she whirled into their lives and upset it all.

She didn't have the sense God gave a gnat sometimes. All she knew about human nature had been learned as a special agent. As an investigator.

Damn, she should have just listened to those who had warned her. Somewhere in her muddled head it should have occurred to her that she might be hurting, not helping.

Instead she had blithely come out here, expecting Dom to feel as passionate as she about justice, and in the process she'd disturbed his peace and had his kids thinking about their mom again, a mom they could probably hardly remember.

Maybe she needed sensitivity training. Or something.

And maybe she'd better get the hell out of here as soon as they got the horses down the mountain.

The afternoon passed swiftly. Courtney decided to watch from the cabin's porch, sitting on a wooden chair. In no way did she want to create any more comparisons for Dom or the boys to deal with.

So she kept the coffee hot on the woodstove, held a mug of her own to keep warm as the day began to cool down and watched.

The boys were indeed helpful, but it still seemed to her the dogs did most of the work. Dogs and boys clearly enjoyed themselves, and from time to time one of the boys would wave at her and she waved back.

The horses didn't seem inclined to be difficult, either. They knew the ropes, evidently, and the youngsters followed the herd obligingly.

Once the horses were all penned, the boys watched from their mounts and Dom went over them one by one, sweeping his hands everywhere, checking every hoof, sometimes pulling a tool from his pocket to pry something loose, or shave a hoof a bit.

What got to her, sadly enough, was watching him run his hands over those horses. He took off his gloves to do it, as if he wouldn't be able to detect things well enough through a thick layer of leather. All she could think of was those hands running over her.

She didn't fight off the images, or the heat they evoked in her. It seemed like too much effort when it was just a fantasy.

And then she had the ridiculously sappy and uncharacteristic thought that it would be nice if someone cared for her the way Dom cared for his horses and his sons.

So maybe Dom wasn't the only one who was getting disturbed by her visit. Evidently she was as well. Thoughts like these had never occurred to her before. Not usually, anyway.

Closing her eyes, though, she could remember the times that Mary had spoken of Dom, of the ranch, of missing her boys. The love had been so apparent. Maybe she had felt a few twinges even back then.

A few.

But now an ugly thought reared its head and she jumped up, going inside.

Had she come here because she wanted what Mary had had? Or because she wanted to see if the stories Mary had told were true? That such a love was possible?

No.

As sure as she was standing here now, the thoughts felt so alien she was certain, absolutely certain, that they'd never occurred to her before. At any level.

So where had that ugliness come from? Guilt? Probably. She sure had enough to feel guilty about, from disturbing this family with her suspicions, to feeling such an attraction to Dom.

Well, attraction was normal and natural. She couldn't help feeling it. What she could help was how she acted on it, and she was determined not to act on it at all.

As for the other, well, she'd already disturbed Dom and maybe the boys. She couldn't undo that. But she could finish the research she had come to do, and get out of here as soon as possible so they could all get back to normal.

She was standing near the stove, soaking up the heat until her skin almost burned, staring blindly as she tried to sort out her emotional confusion. And worse, the heat evoked memories of a hotter climate, another place, ugliness so horrifying even pictures couldn't fully convey it.

She had her own desert ghosts, too, and while she had thought them largely quiet now, apparently they still lurked, ready to freeze her in a pit of awful memory. Or maybe that threatening email had set this off, reminding her anew of what had happened to Mary, of what she suspected.

They couldn't follow her here. Could they?

No. Absolutely not.

She heard the cabin door creak open, but didn't move. Probably one of the boys, she thought, but she needed to find her center before she could interact with them. They needed a calm, cheerful presence, not someone who at the moment would find it difficult to smile.

"Something wrong?"

Dom's voice startled her and she turned to see him standing in the open door.

"No," she answered. "Well, yes."

He stepped inside and closed the door.

"The boys?" she asked immediately.

"They're tending the horses. We just unsaddled them, and I need some coffee."

At once she stepped away from the stove to give him access to the pot. He didn't go for a mug, though. Instead he came straight toward her, pulling off his gloves. God, he smelled good, of fresh air, horses and man. Then he reached out and with one fingertip under her chin he tipped her face up so he could study it.

"What's going on?"

She sighed but didn't try to look away. "I'm kicking myself."

"For what?"

"I came barreling out here without a thought for how this would affect you. I just wanted my answers and justice. I should have thought of your feelings about this."

"My feelings are just fine. On the other hand, yours don't seem to be."

"I'm just wondering what exactly I'm doing."

His rugged face softened just a bit. "You're doing what you need to do. You're being yourself. Don't worry about me. I'm fine."

"Are you? Are you really? It can't be easy for you having

me here like a constant reminder. It must have hurt when the boys brought up Mary at lunch, saying she never did this with you."

"No, not really. She didn't do this kind of thing. Oh, she'd help me muck out stalls when she had the time, and she loved to ride, but taking a couple of days to come up here and gather horses? Not but once or twice. She didn't have the time. I'm not saying she didn't help, because she did, but she had a career of her own, and when the boys were little she had to stay and take care of them." He sighed quietly. "And the boys hardly remember her. They saw her on Skype, they saw her in videos and photos, but they only knew her for a month each year when she'd come home. That's not a lot of memories."

"No. It's sad."

"Actually, for them it might be easier. They didn't notice the great big gaping hole as much as I did. And frankly, I dealt with a lot of that when she went to Iraq, long before she died. I lived with that hole for a long, long time."

"What are you saying?"

"That maybe I've been grieving for longer than two years." He shrugged one shoulder. "Her chair was empty a lot longer than that. I missed her for years, and believe me, phone calls, videos and photos don't make up for it."

Courtney bit her lip, wondering if she was understanding him correctly. "Are you...angry?"

"I was at times. I'm only human. I still get mad at times."

"I think that's normal."

"Of course it's normal." He gave her a crooked smile. "I supported her. I supported her need to do what she did. But that doesn't mean I never got mad at her for leaving the boys and leaving me. Understanding doesn't mean you're always going to be happy about it."

"Of course not."

"So if I can handle all that, I can handle you poking around trying to get what you need."

"I'll be out of your hair soon."

"Who said I wanted that?"

Then he astonished her, absolutely dumfounded her, by slipping his arms around her and hugging her close.

It was just a hug. Nothing more. But in an instant she became aware of his hard, wiry frame, of the muscles hidden beneath denim and other clothing. She was surrounded by his scents, by his arms, by his strength, and her throat grew so tight it felt as if it were wrapped in wire. And heat, delicious heat, pooled heavily between her legs.

Had anything ever felt so good? Not in her memory could she recall ever feeling like this. Sheltered, protected, cared about. And more. A sexual awareness that was quite new in her experience. Not that she'd never been attracted before. But this was somehow different.

Maybe because this man was different. She'd never met anyone quite like him before, with such a quiet strength and so much comfort with life and with himself.

Sure, he said he got angry at Mary at times. He would have been less than human if he had not. But basically he seemed to accept that life had rhythms, good and bad, and he seemed far more able than she to just go with the flow.

"I fight," she said finally, her cheek resting against his shoulder. "I always fight. You don't."

"Some things you can fight. Others, well, it's just a waste of energy. You need to do this."

She bit her lip again as she felt him raise his hand and give just the lightest stroke to her hair. She had left it down this morning, and the touch felt so good she could have purred. Or could have cried.

"So you really don't hate me for coming here?"

"Hell, no. It was a bit of a shock, but I'm long past it."

"Well, I'll be gone soon and you can get back to normal."

"Actually, I was hoping you wouldn't get out of here quite so quick."

She tensed, hardly believing what she heard. Finally she asked, almost breathlessly, "What do you mean?"

"That I was hoping you could stay through next weekend at least. I thought I'd take you up to see the elk migration. It won't be a huge deal, but we might see a few on their way to Colorado. We'll surely see some pronghorns."

She felt at once gladdened and frightened. And she didn't know what to say.

"Just think about it," he said. "It's fun. The boys won't be going, though."

"No?"

"Their grandparents already asked to take them for the weekend. They've got some kind of day trip planned. But the boys aren't all that fascinated anyway."

"Why not?"

"It's boring for them. They have to sit still too long."

At that a weak laugh escaped her. "I'm still wondering how they sit still in school."

"It ain't easy, from what their teachers say. Anyway, given a choice between sitting in the bushes to look for an elk or three, or some pronghorns, they'll choose their grandparents every time."

He gave her a gentle squeeze, then stepped back. She almost hated how bereft she felt.

"Now for that coffee. And you think about next weekend."

"I will."

He filled his mug, pushed his gloves more firmly into his hip pocket and headed for the door.

She stopped him. "Whose clothes am I wearing?"

He looked back, smiling faintly. "My mother's. I couldn't bear to keep Mary's clothes around. They wouldn't have fit you anyway."

Then he vanished, closing the door behind him.

And she stood there feeling somehow that she'd just been through an earthquake. And knowing that something inside her had just somehow been changed forever.

Chapter 8

Twilight came early. The boys wanted to build a fire in the fire pit near the cabin but Dom refused.

"Come here," he said, squatting in the browning grasses near the pit. They both obediently went to him and squatted in perfect imitation of him.

Dom pulled up some grass. "Feel how it cracks in your fingers? It's tinder. A spark would set it off."

Both Todd and Kyle plucked some grass and broke it between their fingers.

"Feel it?" Dom asked. Two young heads bobbed in agreement. "If I build a fire out here, even if I keep it small, I can't be sure a spark wouldn't escape and make a wildfire. So we're not going to even risk it."

He straightened. "Grab a couple of handfuls of grass. I'll show you what I mean."

The boys each pulled up two handfuls and followed Dom to

the cabin. Courtney tagged along, enjoying this and wondering what he planned.

Inside, he went to the woodstove where the fire had burned low. He pulled the ash bucket over. "Now I'm going to take some ash out of the stove."

"Like when you clean it," Todd said knowledgeably.

"Right, but just a shovelful."

He opened the stove door, picked up a small, long-handled shovel and scooped some ash into the bucket. Just a little bit.

Then he carried the bucket a small distance away from the stove, but not near anything flammable.

"How hot does it feel?"

Both boys leaned toward the bucket. "Not very hot," they agreed.

"But even though this is ash, there are still cinders in it, the kind of thing that flies up from a fire. You know what I mean. Now give me some of that grass and stand back."

Todd handed over his two fistfuls, which both fit in the palm of Dom's large hand.

He threw it onto the ash and the effect was almost instantaneous. A puff of flame burst up.

"Oh, cool!" Kyle said.

"Now yours," Dom said, holding out his hand. More grass went into the bucket and flashed immediately into flame. "And that," he continued, "is why we're not going to build a fire outside tonight."

Courtney sat at the table, smiling, watching the boys talk about what they'd just seen. Dom joined her and she turned to him. "That was a brilliant way to handle it."

"Don't applaud me. My dad gave me the same demonstration once. Ranchers hate wildfire with a passion for obvious reasons. And of course, when you have a fire, people have to risk their lives to protect livestock and property."

"You had a good dad, I take it?"

"Both my parents were great. I was lucky. Very down-to-earth folks. The rhythms of nature got into my blood early. In fact, I still remember my dad telling me when I was five or six that if I just listened to the horses, they'd be my best teachers."

"That's a different way of looking at it."

"Not around my place." He gave a quiet laugh. "They can't teach you everything, but they can sure teach you a lot."

He looked over toward the boys. "You want to get the dogs? They need to eat and it's going to be cold tonight. Maybe they'll want to stay inside."

As it happened, they came in just long enough to scarf down three bowls of kibble, then pawed at the door to be let out again. They really *did* like being with the horses. That amused Courtney.

Dinner was a simple meal made on the woodstove: canned soup and crackers, served on chipped and crazed crockery that looked almost as old as the cabin.

Courtney was treated like a princess. When she offered to help with the cleanup, the boys refused. Apparently they wanted to show off their skills for dealing with inconveniences, which included pumping water and heating it on the stove.

Courtney enjoyed the show, and she especially liked the way the boys were so willing to pitch in. She wondered if all kids were helpful at that age.

"So far as I know," Dom answered as they settled again at the table. "Give them a few years. We'll see what happens when they're teens."

"We'll still help," Todd announced. "Everyone helps on a ranch."

Dictum of the day, Courtney thought with amusement. "Well, I've been the least help of all."

"That's okay," Kyle assured her. "You're new."

"Yeah," Todd agreed. "We gotta train you."

"Have to," Dom corrected gently. "That word *gotta* gets too much use."

"It's all-purpose," Courtney said, laughing. "Come on, Dad, don't you know?"

"It seems to cover every base," he agreed, his eyes twinkling. "I think right now we gotta play some Monopoly or Scrabble. Lady's choice."

Kyle scowled. "She's gonna want *words.*"

"Gonna is another overused non-word," Dom said. "Maybe you *need* some Scrabble."

"Da-ad!"

"Monopoly is fine by me," Courtney hastened to say. "I was born to be a millionaire."

The boys scoffed, and it soon turned out that when it came to the board game, they knew exactly how to turn the screws. By the light of a couple of kerosene lanterns, they proved their skills.

"Future billionaires of America," Courtney grumbled jokingly as she paid Kyle rent yet again.

"Nah," Kyle said. "I don't need billions. I need hundreds."

Courtney eyed his stack of play money. "You've got more than a few right now. In fact, you have all of mine and most of your dad's."

"I have some, too," Todd announced. Then he giggled as his dad ruffled his hair.

"Killer instincts," Dom said. "How much money does a horse need?"

Todd snorted. "None. But you need it to take care of them."

Courtney spoke. "So you want to be a rancher like your dad?"

"We both do," Todd answered confidently. "We like the horses."

"I do, too," Courtney agreed. "I never got to spend much time with them, and I'm learning a lot here."

"We can teach you a whole lot more," Kyle announced. "Lots more."

"I'm sure you can. I'm looking forward to it." As soon as she spoke, she wondered if that was a mistake. She looked at Dom, but his face revealed nothing, even though she had just virtually made a promise to the boys. Maybe he didn't freight it with as much significance as she could hear in the words when she mentally replayed them.

Before she could ponder any longer though, Dom announced, "Bedtime. We have an early morning."

The boys had other plans. They wanted a bedtime story and one of them had tucked a favorite book in with their clothes. Courtney was amazed when they asked her to read it to them.

She immediately looked at Dom, wondering if that would trouble him, to see another woman doing something Mary would have done. If he felt she was trespassing too far into intimacy with the boys.

He merely brought a lantern over for her to read by, and returned to the table to sip coffee.

The story was humorous, and at first the boys laughed gleefully. The chuckles grew sleepier though, and more infrequent, until she finally looked up to see they had both fallen sound asleep.

"Tuckered out," Dom murmured. "It's been a busy day."

He moved the lantern back to the table, then went to one of the cots and got a blanket which he draped around her shoulders. "If you want to talk, let's go outside so we don't wake them."

She felt far from ready for sleep, and the chance to sit

outside and watch the stars while talking with Dom was appealing. She dropped the book on the table, clutched the blanket, and followed him out.

The porch chairs weren't that comfortable, but given what she had learned tonight, she imagined no one considered that really necessary. Most likely whoever stayed here overnight came up to work and probably didn't much feel like admiring the night.

The air up here held a cold nip that made her glad for the blanket she had wrapped around her. "I haven't seen so many stars in a long time." She avoided mentioning the Middle East, the last place she had been with areas dark enough to actually see the full glory of the night sky.

"Too many city lights?" he asked.

"Yeah." She looked around. "It isn't often in the modern world that you get a chance to appreciate just how dark a night can really be."

"Moonrise will take care of that soon. Does it make you uneasy?"

"No, but I wouldn't want to try walking across the meadow right now."

He chuckled quietly. "I generally avoid overnight trips when we won't have a moon for that very reason. Next weekend, if you decide you want to watch the migration, we'll still have a quarter moon. It'll be enough."

"I do want to see the migration." There, she'd committed to it. Unfortunately, she wasn't sure if that made her happier, or more nervous. But this world he was showing her was beautiful, and she was reluctant to leave it. Heck, she was even developing a little place in her heart for the boys, and would miss them when she left. Attachments were growing, after only a couple of days.

Maybe she should reverse her decision?

But somehow she couldn't. She tipped her head back,

drinking in the diamond dust of stars strewn on the endlessly deep black of the night sky. "You forget there are so many stars."

"I suppose you can, if you don't see them."

"I used to get myself to sleep at night by imagining that I was falling into stars."

"Yeah?"

"Yeah. Even as a kid I sometimes had trouble falling asleep, but if I could imagine myself falling through stars, *really* falling, I'd be asleep in minutes."

"That's interesting. Guess I'm lucky. Sleep usually conks me right over the head the instant my head touches the pillow."

"Usually?"

"Well, I *can* be distracted."

She caught her breath. Did that mean what it sounded like? Was he flirting? Trying to make her think of forbidden images, forbidden feelings? No, not likely, she told herself. He couldn't possibly feel the kind of attraction for her that she felt for him. In fact, most men seemed to find her intimidating, and some even called her bossy. Part of the kind of job she had, she supposed. Take control. Take charge. Occupy the driver's seat.

She had barely started breathing again, when once again he caused her to stop by simply reaching out to take her hand. His palm was warm, callused, big, and his fingers wrapping around hers felt so good. She held her breath and didn't dare move.

For long minutes there was no sound except an occasional stirring among the horses, the whisper of the night breeze in the treetops, occasional rustling from the woods around them.

"See there?" he said. "Look to your left. Through the trees. You can see a glow."

It took her a few seconds, but finally she realized there was a lightening. "The moon?"

"Yup. Just watch. It happens pretty quickly."

A different kind of dawn, she thought. Pale light slowly brightened, bringing the treetops into relief and then silvering the meadow bit by bit.

"It's always beautiful," he murmured, and for the first time she realized how close he leaned. She could even feel the warm whisper of his breath against her cheek. "So different from sunrise, especially out here where there's almost no pollution. In the morning the light has warmth, but at night it's cold and pure in a different way. Light without heat."

A pleasurable shiver ran through her, and she hoped it didn't reach her hand. But maybe it had, because his grip tightened just a bit.

She tried to find something to say, because the magic he was working on her with his gentle handhold and his quiet voice so near her ear, were likely to make her do something she wasn't sure would be good for either of them.

Finally she grasped at the first barely coherent thought that occurred to her. "Imagine what it must have been like for our ancestors at night. Waiting for moonrise, the whole world around them dark and mysterious."

"I'm pretty sure they stuck close to the fire."

"Probably." A quiet little laugh escaped her. "One minute you're almost poetic, and the next you're prosaic."

"I'm a prosaic kind of guy. Does that bother you?"

"No. Why would it? I just noticed the contrast."

"I have my moments, but mostly I'm just practical to the core. I have to be."

"I suppose you do. So if we were cave dwellers, we'd be sitting close to the fire rather than out here enjoying the night's beauty."

"Only because their nights must have been so much more

threatening. But we have dogs and horses. One or the other would alert us."

"True. It's handy to have animal friends."

"They're more than friends. They're partners."

She nodded, liking the sound of that. "All my life, dogs were just someone's pets. I don't mean that I wasn't aware of working dogs. I just never saw it up close and personal before."

"They impress the hell out of *me,* and I've been around herders my entire life. I'm impressed not just by what they can do so naturally, but by the intense focus they get when they're working. You couldn't distract them with a meaty bone then."

"That *is* amazing."

"So move our cave people forward in time to when they had dogs to keep watch."

"They probably slept a lot better."

"That would be my guess. In fact, it would be my guess that wolves may have adopted people and not the other way around. We're wasteful. Imagine our garbage heaps."

That drew a real laugh from her. "Even in tight times we still manage to waste something, it seems."

"Yup. Even hunter-gatherers had to leave something behind."

She dared to turn her head so she could see his face. The moonlight, especially on the shadowed porch, made him look mysterious. "You know a lot about this?"

"I read a lot. Mostly nonfiction."

"But not just about horses and ranching?"

"Some about horses, but most of what I know about them comes from experience and generations of knowledge that were handed down to me. My people were always horse people."

She put on a mock investigator's face. "Can you prove that? Do you have the genealogical information?"

He chuckled. "Actually, yes. This family and horses go back at least three hundred years. Grooms, mainly, in the old days, until my great-grandfather settled out here around 1920."

"Your family has done well."

"Well enough. We take care of the land and the horses. And maybe when we're gone, we'll leave only a small footprint."

"That's an unusual way to look at it."

He gave a slight shake of his head. "My dad and granddad always told me that if you respect and care for nature, nature will take care of you."

"That's what you were trying to show the boys tonight with the dry grass."

"In part. We live very close to nature here, Courtney. We aren't walled off from it by concrete and pavement. A stray spark, a bad storm, a drought, a disease… Those things have a strong and pretty immediate impact on us."

"I can see they would."

"It's not an easy life, but it's a good one."

She wondered if that was some kind of warning, and if so where it had come from. But even as the thought crossed her mind, she realized he had moved closer. An instant later, his lips touched hers. Just a light, tentative brush.

"Dom…" What? What was she going to say when she wanted him to kiss her? Wanted it like mad.

"Shh," he said. His free hand cupped her cheek and the back of her neck, holding her gently as he moved in for another kiss, a real one this time. His mouth covered hers, warm and amazingly gentle. She resisted for an instant, but only an instant as desire and need swamped her. Too fast, entirely too fast, he drew back a few inches.

"I think," he said huskily, "that we need to consider whether to explore that any further." Then he brushed his lips lightly against hers once more and pulled back, releasing her hand.

"Early morning," he reminded her.

She had more than a little to think about as she followed him back into the cabin. And a surprising amount of it scared her.

Dom lay awake in his cot, holding perfectly still, wondering if he had lost his mind. If he was even going to consider the possibility of getting involved again, then it seemed to him he ought to be looking at women who already lived around here, women who didn't have careers other than ranching.

He'd done that once, and the price had been grief. And not just grief because Mary had died, but the grief that came along with having her gone so much. There was no question in his mind that Courtney would want to continue her job, and it would take her far from Conard County. How could it not?

On the other hand, there was a widow two ranches over who'd cast her eye his way a couple of times. She was pretty, had a son of her own slightly older than his boys, and knew how to operate a ranch. Was devoted to it, in fact. She was someone he could chat with about some of the things that interested him when they met at the feed store or after church on a Sunday, when he made it.

That would make sense.

What he was feeling now did not.

Or maybe it just fit with his nature. Part of what had attracted him to Mary to begin with was that she wasn't all about ranching and horses all of the time. She had other things to talk about, interesting things that carried him out of his absorption.

Maybe that was part of what was pulling him here: an intersection with a life very different from his own.

Damn, he thought, maybe he needed to get out and about more, away from the horse community where he did probably ninety percent of his socializing. Maybe the attraction he was feeling was nothing but a window to a different world.

Then he remembered the kiss, and his loins stirred, and he knew he was looking for reasons for something that didn't have reasons.

Courtney might not have appeared to be his type at first look, but apparently she was very much his type in some important ways.

And the boys liked her.

He rolled over and forced his eyes closed, trying to ignore the humming in his body that insisted on reminding him Courtney was only a few feet away.

Thank God the boys were here.

But what about next weekend?

At the thought of taking Courtney out to see the migrations, he had the worst urge to pound his fist on his pillow. Alone with her on an overnight camping trip? Was he losing his mind?

Did he have the willpower to keep his hands to himself? He wished she'd pulled away from his kiss, wished she'd been shocked or disturbed. Instead she had welcomed him, for however brief a time.

He'd seen the flush in her cheeks, the darkening of her eyes a couple of times when that awareness had suddenly crackled between them like lightning before a storm.

He had known she was attracted, yet he'd been an idiot and reached for her hand out there on the porch. And he'd been even more of an idiot when he kissed her.

The image of his lesson to the boys sprang to his mind. He was playing with tinder here and he ought to know better. This could hurt someone. This could change lives forever, and not necessarily in a good way. He needed to think about all the problems, not just the urges. Problems like his boys, problems like her career. Problems like the fact that they came from entirely different worlds. At least Mary had been local. She hadn't suffered culture shock by marrying him.

Marriage? Whoa. Too early to even think about that. No, he needed to think about the inherent risks in having a relationship with a woman who was leaving to go back to her job in Georgia. Never in his life had he been capable of a fling.

Never. It wasn't his nature. It was girlfriends who always jilted him. He was always the fool who wound up with the broken heart. Loyalty was rooted deep in his nature, and flings were beyond him. He'd never been able to just satisfy an urge without getting involved.

So what did he do? He kissed the worst possible woman.

Oh, man, he was digging the hole deeper with everything he did. Digging deeper and, if he were to be honest with himself, with absolutely no desire to stop.

Yet, anyway.

Chapter 9

In the morning, just as the first pale rays of sunlight were poking above the trees, Courtney headed for the outhouse. It was set a fair distance from the cabin, probably for sanitary reasons, and she took her time wandering the well-trodden path.

After she finished, she headed toward the cabin, soaking up the brightening day and chilly air. Nearby, trees began to stir as the air warmed. It was going to be a gorgeous day.

The peace shattered in an instant, with a recognizable gunshot. Instinctively she fell to the ground and remained motionless. At once she was back in Iraq, where such sounds always meant death. She dug her fingers into the dirt, battling to remember where she was.

The door of the cabin flew open and she saw Dom, a shotgun in hand, scanning the area. His gaze fell on her.

"Are you okay?"

"Yeah." But with adrenaline now rushing through her, what

she most wanted was to leap to her feet and go hunt that shooter down. Moving one arm, she instinctively felt for her gun, and she started calculating the fastest, safest route to the trees. Unfortunately, even as she wanted to take action, she simultaneously realized she didn't have her gun and that she had no idea where that gunshot had come from. Between the trees and the surrounding mountains it could have come from anywhere. "Dom, get back inside."

He ignored her, of course.

"Damn hunters," Dom muttered. "My land is posted, but that never keeps them away."

He lifted his head and shouted. "No deer here. Shoot again and I'll hunt you down!"

Silence filled the morning, except for the uneasy stirring of the horses. Gradually other sounds returned.

"I'm moving now," Dom called.

"No, Dom," Courtney cried. "Don't move!"

But he ignored her, making his way swiftly to Courtney's side. Before he got to her, she rose to a crouch, looking around. "Damn it," she said between her teeth, "Dom, you don't have the sense God gave a gnat." If he wasn't going to stay out of the line of fire, she would damn well make him.

"Dad?"

"Stay inside, Kyle."

Dom, shotgun at ready, reached her and tucked her close to his side, ignoring her quiet cussing as they hurried back to the cabin.

"Damn hunters," he said again as they entered the cabin. "Every single year some idiot shoots without looking."

"You don't know it was a hunter."

He caught her eye. "Do *you* know something you're not telling me?"

"No! It's my training, my experience in Iraq. You should never just assume something like that."

"Well, this isn't Iraq," he said logically enough. "So unless you have some reason to think someone wants to take a potshot at you, then it's a hunter."

She caught his drift, saw his glance at the boys. They were both standing in their nightclothes, wide-eyed.

"It was a hunter," she agreed tensely.

"Then the smart thing to do is make breakfast while he finds some other place to look for deer."

As her adrenaline subsided, Courtney took a seat. "He may not have even been shooting at me."

"Probably not," Dom agreed. "Sound echoes off these hills."

"Yeah. I'm sure."

"Did someone shoot at Courtney, Dad?" Todd spoke, but both boys' eyes had grown huge.

Courtney looked at the frightened boys, and her heart and gut both twisted. "No, of course not." She couldn't bear the thought of what might have occurred to them, after what had happened to their mother.

"Of course not," Dom said firmly. "It was some hunter. He might not even have been aiming this way."

"They're not supposed to hunt here," Kyle said.

"No, they're not. But some people don't pay attention to signs and fences. Now let's get breakfast started."

Courtney was watching the boys closely, and felt relief when they seemed to relax. She'd better not run across that hunter, because if she did he was going to get an earful for the fright he had given these boys. One hell of an earful.

But later, while the boys were eating at the table, Dom drew her back outside under the pretext of drinking their coffee on the porch.

"Are you sure that no one is after you?" he asked.

It was a fair question after her reaction this morning. No

matter how she sorted it in her head, she thought it more likely that if someone wanted to get her, they would wait until she returned to Georgia. Especially since absolutely no one could know where she was right now.

"I'm sure. At least for now. I told you, my response came from my training. If someone wanted to get me, they'd have to be foolhardy to try it here. And it would cause them unnecessary trouble when they could get me far easier on the streets at home."

After a moment he nodded. "It was a hunter. Had to be. It's not like you're alone up here."

"That's right. If someone was hunting me, it'd just make it unnecessarily messy and noisy if you and the boys were around." She sighed, trying to let go of a creeping uneasiness. "Frankly, Dom, I don't think these guys are quite that stupid. If they want me dead, it'll happen at a place and a time that will look like something else entirely. Like with Mary." It almost killed her to speak those last three words.

Dom winced, just a bit, then said, "Like a hunting accident?"

"Not when I'm not alone."

After a few seconds of thought, he nodded. "Okay. I'm inclined to agree with you."

"Besides, there are plenty of ways they can stop me without killing me. They've succeeded for two years now. Like you said, I have no idea where that shot came from, or even if it was aimed anywhere near me."

He appeared to accept that. "You'd better eat something before we head back."

But she noticed he stood on the porch by himself for a while, scanning the hills around them. Then he seemed to shake free of his thoughts, and when he came back inside he seemed settled in his own mind.

* * *

Dom tied the packhorse's lead rein to the back of Courtney's saddle. "You ride in the middle of the herd."

"What? Why?"

"Just do it. Stay in the middle. We'll keep things moving all around you."

That's when she realized he wasn't completely certain that had been a random shot. That he was worried about a repetition. And it wasn't the twins he was worried about.

Her stomach burned a bit. "You're overreacting," she told him. "No one knows where I am."

"Maybe not. But let's not test it, okay?"

Something in his face, maybe anger, maybe worry, made her shut up and do as told.

Surprising, to Courtney at least, was the way the horses headed home. Even after a summer in the high pasture where they had been able to roam free, they seemed eager to go down the mountain. Maybe because they had learned it would be warmer below and they would get more attention.

Of course, what did she know about what a horse would think?

But there were surprisingly few problems. The dogs kept the herd together, along with Dom and the boys, who rode around the edges of the gathering. Everybody except her seemed familiar with the drill.

She realized the thing that amazed her most was the way it all went off like clockwork: man, boys, dogs, horses, all cooperating.

The trail home was a lot broader and smoother than the climb they had made yesterday. When a stream cut in alongside them, Dom let the herd and their mounts pause to drink as they chose, then with a few commands started the whole band moving again with the aid of the dogs.

Courtney could see the dogs were the most important of

his helpers, but in no way did he make the boys feel as if they mattered less, even though it was clear even to her untutored eyes that they were still learning. In fact, their horses may have been in more charge of what they were doing than the boys.

Hadn't one of them said just last night that Marti would tell her what to do?

And Marti seemed to understand without any instruction at all that her role in this was to simply walk along in the midst of all the bustle and movement. She never tried to join in the activity of the boys and Dom.

Which was good, because a few times, the way the boys' and Dom's horses wheeled sharply to corral laggers or wanderers, she was sure she would have been unseated if Marti had tried that.

The herd picked up pace as the ranch came in view. Marti tried to keep up and Courtney found her sudden trot a bit uncomfortable as she lifted and fell in the saddle. Following Dom's directions, she pressed into the stirrups and forward. Marti slowed immediately, but tossed her head as if she didn't like it.

"Sorry, girl," Courtney said. "I'm still not good at this."

Whether she liked it or not, though, Marti slowed to a smooth walk and Courtney felt secure again. She leaned forward a bit to pat the mare's neck in approval. Up ahead she could see Ted opening a gate to a large corral across from the pasture where the rest of the herd waited, clearly watching. So these horses weren't going to the same pasture. Why?

There was no time to ask right then. Dom let out a couple of whistles, and the dogs, who had mostly been trotting along behind the horses, spread out and began to steer them toward the open gate. The boys took their cue from the dogs, adding their presence to ease the moving herd from a cluster to more of a line. One or two at a time, the horses entered the corral.

By the time Courtney caught up, all the horses were safely penned. The morning, which had been full of the drum of hoofbeats, the whistles of man and boys, and the barks of dogs, had grown quiet except for the snorting of the penned horses and the occasional sound of them pawing at the ground.

Dom trotted over to her and pulled his mount up beside her. He looked happy. "How are you doing?"

"I'm fine. Actually, I'm amazed at how well that went."

The corners of his eyes crinkled. "You expected a stampede?"

"I just never dreamed it could go so easily."

"The important thing is to never let it get out of control. And my older mares know the pattern anyway. Forage was getting lean up there. They know it's time to come down here where there'll be more food."

"Why did you pen them separately?"

"Need to check for disease and deworm them before I put them in with the rest."

He reached out and laid his hand over one of hers. "Ready to head for the barn?"

She was indeed. Riding was an unaccustomed activity, and while she'd been only slightly sore after yesterday's ride, she had a feeling it was going to be worse today as the unusual use of muscles compounded.

Dom reached over and took her lead rein. "Just relax. Marti knows the drill. I'll keep her from taking off like a bat out of hell."

"Would she do that?"

"She likes the barn a lot after she works for a couple of days." He winked. "All that TLC plus some oats? Who could resist?"

"Certainly not me," Courtney said with a laugh. She tossed

her head, loving the way the dry air and sunshine felt. "I could get addicted to this. I had a whole lot of fun."

She felt a little stiff when they dismounted in the barn. The guys tethered the horses in grooming stalls. Ted and Dom did all the unsaddling but then Courtney got her first lessons in grooming.

Marti clearly loved being curried. Her flanks rippled under the brush even as she stood stock-still for the attention. Occasionally she lowered her head to munch some oats or straw, or drink from the large pail.

"You're doing great," Dom said, entering the stall with her. "Marti loves you."

"How can you tell?"

"Take a look at her. She couldn't be more relaxed. I think you just got yourself a horse."

Courtney laughed, not taking it seriously. How could she have a horse when she was leaving soon? But the idea touched her anyway. She gave Marti a couple of additional pats and continued brushing while Dom checked her hooves. Then he took another brush and worked on Marti's tail.

"Thanks," Courtney said. "I'm not sure I'm ready to stand behind her."

"You'll notice I'm standing a bit to the side here. Marti may trust us, but she's also got instincts. No point in stirring them up."

"You think a lot about what the horses like and don't like."

"Sure I do. They matter, too."

"I haven't had the opportunity to think much about things like that."

"Never had a pet?"

"Not since I was very little. A cat."

"That's too bad. Animals have a lot to teach us."

"Probably a lot of it nicer than people."

"And maybe you've got a skewed view of people, given your job."

She paused, holding stock-still, anger rising in her. "What do you know about my job?"

"Sorry." He looked up from combing Marti's tail. "I didn't mean that to sound judgmental. Just that I figure you must see a lot of the worst side of people."

"I see a lot of the good side, too."

"I believe you."

Almost muscle by muscle, she released her irritation and relaxed. "Sorry. I don't know why I'm feeling so defensive."

"It's okay. I was making assumptions I had no right to make."

"Maybe your assumptions are correct," she said after a moment. "I came out here looking for something bad, and instead I found something good. Yesterday and today...well, they've been idyllic for me."

"We're not always idyllic. I've got this theory, though."

"What's that?"

"When you work hard with your body, your mind finds more peace."

She resumed brushing Marti with slow strokes as she pondered that. "You may be right. Before I went to the CRFO, I had to spend a lot of time working the kinks out every night."

"Meaning?"

"I had to jog long distances or work out at a gym. I needed to unwind. Today I feel like I'm unwound just fine."

He chuckled quietly. "We're lucky here. We don't have a lot, but we have what we need, and plenty of work to fill a day. I'm even hoping the sale will go well enough next month that I can hire another hand. Ted's been with us forever, but in better times we used to have someone to help him out. These days, ranches around here are sharing hands."

"How do you do that?"

"I put out a call that I need a certain number of guys for a particular kind of work. My neighbors send over their hands. Kind of like a labor pool. Sometimes Ted goes to help out on other ranches."

"I take it the heyday of the cowboy is over?"

"Not totally. But it never paid well to begin with. Used to be you'd hire a guy for less than three hundred a month, give him grub, a place to sleep and a horse to ride. He had to provide his own saddle. People won't work that way anymore, and I don't blame them."

"You're killing my fantasies."

"Sorry. I know some ranches that bring in *vaqueros*, cowboys, from Mexico for seasonal work, but I don't need to do that, and I'd feel like I was taking advantage of them anyway."

"But if they want the work…"

"They do." He gave the horse's tail another swipe, then dropped it. "But I'd still feel like I was taking advantage. I'd rather pay the guys who live around here a decent wage for the days they work for me."

"And others feel the same way."

"Obviously. That's how we formed the pool. Now maybe if I was running big cattle herds I'd need to do something different. But I'm more about quality than quantity, so the question isn't one I need to argue with myself about."

"So you breed champions?"

He smiled at her over Marti's back. "It's enough to know I don't have a whole lot of competition in some areas."

Evening settled over the ranch early, but the horses had had their first worming and seemed happy enough to meander around the corral and enjoy the treats of some high-quality feed in between nibbles on the grass.

Dom lingered outside longer than necessary, mainly because he was hiding. The boys were capable of putting out tonight's meal, an assortment of cold cuts and condiments, and were pretty proud of their ability to take charge of making a meal, simple though it was.

But Courtney was in there. And as he'd watched her growing appreciation for the ranch and the kind of work he did, his attraction to her troubled him even more.

This, he reminded himself, was a vacation for her. A change of pace. Not a way of life she'd want to adopt on a permanent basis. Just the thought of her trying to transition from a fast-paced lifestyle to this bucolic one was enough to make him backpedal fast.

Mary hadn't been able to do it, and Mary had grown up on a ranch. She'd needed more excitement and variety, more of a social life, a sense of greater importance than raising horses could give her.

That had been okay then. This was now. He knew all the costs now, that came with bringing someone into your life who couldn't fully *live* your life. There had been gulfs and gaps that they'd never been able to bridge simply because one or the other couldn't fully understand. You could live with that.

It was the other stuff, like being alone for long periods, that had been harder to endure. And finally there had been wrenching, tearing, sundering grief.

He'd have to be an idiot to even think about signing on for something like that again.

So while he watched Courtney's face shine with pleasure in each new thing, and watched her start to slip into the ranch's life, he knew it wouldn't last.

So he didn't want to go back in there. He didn't want to feel that pull, that unreasoning pull, toward her. He didn't want to have to remind himself that when he'd first seen her he'd thought her too thin, too tense. Because as the tension vanished, and her face started to shine with the relaxed outdoor life, he didn't notice that thinness anymore. He didn't notice that her face had sharper lines than he liked.

What he noticed was a blossoming rose, and that was dangerous.

He also didn't want to think that she might be at risk over this obsession of hers. She thought she might get in trouble on her job. She ought to know that wasn't the only threat she faced. If someone had killed Mary over what had happened in Iraq, how could she possibly think it was less likely that they'd react the same way if they found out what she was doing? She of all people ought to know what humans were capable of.

And she'd emailed that picture to a friend. Someone had already tried to warn her off, and now they might have the means of finding her through that email. Maybe. He knew damn all about how such things worked, and maybe he'd seen too many movies.

But while he didn't think he and the boys were at risk, she might well be.

He stiffened a bit as he leaned on the corral fencing. He'd been downplaying the danger, and so had she. It was something neither of them really wanted to look at, but he wasn't the type to stick his head in a hole in the sand. And he couldn't imagine why *she* was doing so. It wasn't as if people didn't get murdered all the time.

What if that shot this morning hadn't just been some hunter? He turned it around in his mind, remembering the sick feeling he'd had when he burst out of the cabin and saw Courtney on the ground. She'd reacted the right way, but his heart had damn near stopped when he saw her laid out flat.

No, it had to have been a hunter. Surely someone who wanted to kill her wouldn't have given up after a single shot? Of course, a second shot would have made it clear it wasn't just some deer hunter, and these mountains would have been swarming with law enforcement pretty quickly. He knew how fast Gage could gather a posse from around here. And then of course there was the problem of witnesses. She was right about that. There were better ways to make something look like an accident than shooting at a woman in the company of others who hadn't been a hundred yards from a horse pen.

Hell.

Turning sharply, he marched back into the house. He found the table deserted, the food left out for him. He could hear the boys upstairs and it sounded like they were getting their stuff together for school in the morning. Cripes, he probably needed to do a load of laundry.

He called up the stairs. "Kyle? Todd?"

Two heads appeared, looking down from the landing. "Yeah?"

"Do you have clean clothes for tomorrow?"

"Yeah," Kyle answered.

"Me, too," Todd agreed.

"Nice clothes? Not something that should be in a rag bin?"

"Clean shirts and jeans."

"Underwear?"

"Check," answered Kyle. He'd heard that on some program or other, and it popped up from time to time.

"Do I need to do laundry tomorrow?"

"Probably," Todd said. "I think this is my last pair of jeans."

"Okay. Make sure everything comes down the laundry chute tonight. And I mean *everything*."

Putting in that laundry chute had been one of his smarter moves. The boys didn't mind using it. In fact, they enjoyed it, so he rarely found dirty clothes lying around up there.

"I'll be up in a minute. I need to talk to Courtney for a second."

"Okay." They disappeared.

He found Courtney in his office, sitting at the boys' computer. She had her chin in her hand, and from what he could tell she was looking at email.

"Anything?" he asked.

"Nope. I wasn't expecting anything so soon. It's a weekend. And my friend might not find anything anyway."

"What did you ask her to do?"

"Just see if that face matched anything in our photo database."

"But you didn't tell her why?"

She lifted her head sharply and swiveled to look at him. "Of course not!"

"Sorry. But I think we've been avoiding a certain possibility here. That if you're right, you might be as much of a threat to someone as Mary was."

"I could be. If I could find anything. If I could build a case from it. At this point, that's damned unlikely."

"Then why are you still pursuing it?"

"Because I have to."

It suddenly struck him that they were practically fighting, and over nothing at all, really. Other than his sudden concern that she might be underestimating the risk to herself.

"Talk to me," he said after a moment. "What if that face comes back to you? What if you find out who it is?"

"Then I have to go to work trying to put pieces together to establish that he could have been one of the rapists. That he had the opportunity and motive to kill Mary."

"After all this time?"

"That's what cold case work is all about. I have evidence. Oh, yes, I have evidence. But what I need most of all is to know who the perpetrator was. That's going to be the hard part and I may never accomplish it. But I have to try."

"Even if it means risking your own neck?"

"Mary wasn't the only victim," she said quietly.

That drew him up short. His hands tightened into fists, then he forced them to relax. "No," he said finally. "No, she wasn't."

Then he turned and stomped upstairs to read to the boys, to talk to them until they fell asleep, which promised to be early after all the work they had done that day. To think about anything except his dead wife and the woman he was worried about now.

Damn it, he'd tried not to care again. He'd been avoiding it like the plague.

Now here he was, giving a damn about something besides his boys and the ranch. Worried again.

So much for learning his lesson.

Chapter 10

Courtney sat at the desk in the small office, wondering what the hell had just happened. Dom had come in here looking all wound up, which was unusual from what she'd seen, but he was certainly wound up now.

About her safety? Was that all it was? The episode had seemed to come out of nowhere after what had been a truly relaxed weekend and it seemed uncharacteristic. But then how well did she know him?

Maybe she should change her mind about the upcoming weekend. It would be easy enough to come up with an excuse and leave this man what little peace he'd managed to find before she'd blithely waltzed into his life and changed it forever with a piece of news he clearly hadn't wanted to know.

She steepled her hands beneath her chin and closed her eyes, thinking. Solving this case was on the outer limits of possibility, but then, most cold cases were. She'd worked on them enough to know.

Still, she had access to the evidence they'd managed to collect in Iraq, good evidence, enough to kick an investigation into high gear. A few more pieces, an identity or two, and she could probably pull it together enough to get a prosecution, if not a conviction.

She needed that, for Mary, for those Iraqi women and for herself.

Even if she never pulled together a prosecutable case, she would at least know she'd done everything, absolutely *everything,* she could for all those women. That mattered.

And she was fairly certain that Dom was overestimating the risk to her, at least at present. If she went home and started the ball rolling, that might be something to worry about, although only a minor worry. If she opened a case against someone, they'd be the first suspect if anything untoward happened to her. That was protection in itself.

She sighed, and wondered if she should just get out of here. Obviously something was working on Dom. Obviously they were both feeling an attraction that neither of them found comfortable. And obviously she'd stirred up Dom's life, calm as he might seem about it.

Maybe it would be better for Dom and his boys if she just hit the road. She could find if that face matched anyone of interest just as well on the road as she could here. It wasn't like she couldn't get email on her phone.

Yes, there was still stuff of Mary's to go through, but she doubted she'd find much more of any use. Mary had been talking and writing to her family, and she wouldn't have said anything about her undercover role. Not a word, because she had absolutely no reason to. She wouldn't want her family to know, she would have believed that she could pass information to Courtney soon enough.

All in all, it had been the height of stupidity to come here. She could feel the corners of her mouth sag as she admitted to herself that she hadn't really thought this through. Usually she calculated every step she took, but this time, acting on an impulse that had been bugging her for two years, she'd come out here and thrown a family into a turmoil on an unreasonable hope that she might find something useful.

Ridiculous. She owed Dom one hell of an apology.

Pushing back from the desk, she rose. She'd heard him come back downstairs and go out onto the front porch. Maybe he was walking off whatever had gotten to him.

Grabbing her jacket, she went to look and found him sitting on the wide front porch, chair tipped back, one booted foot on the railing.

"I'm sorry," she said, shoving her hands into her pockets. Here the moonlight added only a faint glow, and clouds occasionally blacked out the night.

She thought he looked at her. "For what?"

"For barging in, for stirring all this up. Clearly I didn't think it through. I was just driven."

"It's okay."

"No, it's not okay. And something is obviously bugging you. I'll be out of here in the morning."

He didn't move. Not a muscle that she could tell. "Now why would you do that? Decided you don't want to see the migration?"

"It's not that." Not exactly. But going camping overnight with a man who was obviously troubled by her presence here wasn't exactly appealing. Especially when she found *him* so appealing. "But I feel like I'm standing on train tracks," she said finally.

"Why?"

"Because whatever is happening between us is something neither of us seems to want." There, it was out. Part of her wanted to turn and walk away before he could say a word, partly out of embarrassment for being so direct, partly because she feared what he might say. When had she gotten so involved that she cared? Being an investigator had toughened her. Rarely did she care what anyone thought of her as long as she knew she was doing her job correctly.

But somehow this wasn't just a job anymore. That frightened her as much as anything.

"Don't go," he said. "I'm dealing with my own crap, and it's not anything you brought with you."

"But I woke it up."

"Maybe. Yes. It happens. The crap you don't deal with stays stuck to your boot heels for life, so now's as good a time as any to scrape it off."

She hesitated. "I guess that depends on whether you can scrape it off. It's not like I'm not having any issues. I'm actually feeling pretty stupid for coming out here unannounced, so focused on my need to solve this case that I never gave a thought to what pain I might cause you."

"It's an old pain, not a new one. Sometimes you just have to look at things and sort them out."

"Should I ask? Or not."

"I don't know. I'm not clear myself about what's happening. I just know I need to think some things through." He dropped his booted foot to the floor and patted the chair beside him.

She sat, perching almost on the edge of the chair.

"The things I'm feeling," he said slowly, staring into the night, "are things I'm not sure I want to feel."

"This attraction?"

He gave a short laugh. "Yeah. Where does that lead? Nowhere that I can see. Your life is in Georgia, not here. And I'm wondering why I don't have the sense to just shut it down. But what's even harder is that I'm looking at my relationship with Mary in a different way. Thinking that I probably can't do that again."

"Do what again?"

"Get involved with someone who won't be here."

He had a point. "We're far from involved. And I'll hop in my car in the morning if that'll make it easier."

"You keep saying that. But it doesn't help me deal with the past. And that's what I need to deal with. Choices I made, and the consequences. I guess I still need to make peace with some things, because if I don't I'll never move on."

"Was it so hard?"

"From time to time." He sighed and tipped back again, propping one foot against the porch rail. "I loved her, Courtney. And I know lots of families make the same sacrifices. I guess I just didn't realize how much having to do that changed me."

"I can understand that."

"Can you?"

"I may not have any direct experience, but I've talked to enough widows. It's inevitable when you deal with as many military and their families as I do. You meet people who say goodbye to someone they love, over and over again. And you meet those who've just learned that their spouse will never return. It's hard."

"It is," he agreed.

"Are you having regrets?"

"Hell, no. I'll never regret loving Mary. But I'm kind of figuring out that I was angrier than I realized."

"About her going to Iraq?"

"Yes. Logically I get it. She had a higher calling. She couldn't walk away from her unit. I'm sure I don't have to tell you about loyalty to your unit. You probably understand it better than I do.

"I understand it," she agreed.

"Well, I get it in my own way. It'd be like me not taking care of my horses. So Mary had a higher calling really. Higher than mine. Me, I'm just a fancy wrangler. She was a nurse. She took care of *people*. She did important work."

"Very important," Courtney agreed. "She saved lives."

"And I get that. But I guess what I didn't get back then, or wouldn't even let myself think about, was how angry it made me that she left her boys behind."

A ripple of genuine concern passed through Courtney, and she wasn't sure what to say, except, "I've known plenty of parents who feel the same. Maybe it's easier when it's the mom who stays home and the man who goes."

"Are you accusing me of sexism?"

"Not really. But I think it so permeates us as a species that dads go off to do things, and moms stay home with the kids, well…" She hesitated, not wanting to make him angry. Maybe she shouldn't say it at all. He didn't give her the chance.

"You might be right," he said. "You might be right."

"In what way?" Caution had gripped her, making her feel her way carefully.

"Well, I hadn't rearranged the picture in my mind, but I think you're right. I mean, men go off to war, off to oil rigs, off to wherever to do their jobs. But something seems wrong about a woman doing it."

"Especially when she has young children."

"Yup." He almost bit the word off.

Courtney waited silently, knowing this was one of the times she had to let the other person guide the conversation.

"Well, damn," he finally said quietly.

"Damn?"

"I'm an idiot."

"Now that's one thing I don't believe for a minute."

Even in the faint light as another cloud scudded over the moon, she could see him shake his head.

"No, I'm an idiot," he said again. "We had a role reversal in this family, and I thought I accepted it, but I never really thought about the underlying assumptions I had. I spend my time with horses."

"And?"

"And the mares take care of the young. The stallions pretty much ignore the foals and colts unless there's a threat. Then they might step in, but the mares run the show, take care of the young. Stallions are, for the most part, sperm donors and little else."

Courtney couldn't help it. A quiet giggle escaped her.

He turned toward her. "Are you laughing at me?"

"No, at your description. I know a lot of guys who would take umbrage."

"Well, I won't. So here I am, looking at the natural order of things, and realizing I was mad at Mary because she didn't follow the natural order the way I had it figured out. That's idiocy. The kids had two parents. One of them went away on her job. That should be the end of it."

"Maybe that's logical, but not necessarily emotionally true." She hesitated, then said, "One of the subjects I studied in college was anthropology. I kind of got the feeling after a while that women actually ran things, made sure families were fed, all that important stuff. That man-the-hunter was rarely as successful at feeding the tribe as the women who gathered or grew the food. So I had the feeling that maybe women were actually sending men off to do things that would wear them out. Get them out of the camp so they couldn't make trouble."

He surprised her by laughing. "Now there's a view I've never heard before."

"Well, I'm probably wrong. But it seemed like the men in most pre-literate cultures had things to do that pretty much kept them away from agriculture, or gathering, or taking care of kids except for brief periods."

"So you think it's deep-rooted? The idea of women as nurturers and men as being off doing other stuff?"

"Maybe. Regardless, I think even now it's socially more

acceptable for a man to leave his family to go fight or work, and that's got to make it harder when it's the woman who goes and the man who stays home. A very old social contract is broken."

"Hmm."

He fell silent and she let him think. It was growing chilly, so she stuffed her hands deeper into her pockets, staring out into the night. Waiting. Hoping she hadn't made a sore spot sorer.

"That's it," he said finally.

"What?"

"I was doing the modern-man thing, but in reality some-where inside there was a caveman. I was blaming her for abandoning her kids long before she died, and I didn't even know it."

"She didn't abandon them."

"No, she didn't. No more than a sailor who's gone to sea."

"Exactly."

"She had competing imperatives. Two callings. Motherhood and nursing."

"And evidently she felt you were a good enough dad for her to follow her second calling."

"I hadn't thought of it that way."

"Well, you should. She paid you a high compliment. She didn't abandon her kids. She entrusted them to your care while she had to be away. That's a very different thing."

He sighed. "Yeah. It is. How'd my head get so screwed up?"

"You're asking me? I don't think you're screwed up. I just think you didn't have much of a social support system for doing things differently." She hesitated. "I imagine things around here are more traditional, usually."

"Mostly, yes."

"But you bucked tradition and let Mary do what she needed to do. You're a remarkable man."

"That's debatable." He shifted on his chair and it creaked a bit. "Well, that skewed my head around."

"Hidden assumptions can do that. It was one of the things they hit most heavily on in our training. Hidden assumptions can make you blind and frustrate an entire investigation. Which is not to say I never run into any of my own."

"I guess we all have them."

"More than we'll ever know, probably." She was still sitting on the edge of her chair, wondering if she should go inside now, up to bed, or just wait in case he had more he wanted to talk about.

He'd certainly made it clear he didn't want to get involved with someone who was heading back to Georgia. And he was right. She didn't want to get involved with someone who was so firmly rooted to soil thousands of miles from where her life was.

So the smart thing to do… She stopped the thought. Clearly she wasn't doing the smart thing, hadn't been doing it since she'd decided to make this trip. What made her think she was going to start now?

No, she would stay out the week, enjoy life on the ranch and pay the price later.

There was always a price. Leaving tomorrow or leaving later didn't seem to make much difference now. She'd stirred up the hornet's nest, she tasted an attraction she was unwilling to just walk away from. Forbidden fruit.

She was already in too deep. She might as well just enjoy the next week. Besides, once she got back into the swing of things at home, this time would seem like a dream. God knew, she'd experienced that often enough in her travels.

Dom surprised her by asking, "How come you're not married?"

"I've never really looked for that. Anyway, I think I intimidate men."

"You must be meeting the wrong men."

She laughed. "No. I know I'm pushy and even bossy. I don't take crap from anybody, and I like to take charge. You just haven't seen that part of me yet."

"Well, I'm not sure I'd dislike it. Might lead to some rows, though."

"I can guarantee it would."

"So you don't fit the stereotypes in your world, either?"

"Apparently not. It's a very macho world."

"So's this one."

"Not as much, at least not around here." She smiled into the darkness. "You know, it's been nice to get away from all that back home. If you want to know what it feels like to be a fifth wheel, be a woman on a SWAT team. It's not that I can't do it, it's just that they don't *think* I can. And when I do, they act all surprised."

"That must be galling."

"It's the way it is. For all the progress we've made, we still don't seem capable of seeing people as just people. We're always laboring under expectations from hidden assumptions. I don't even think most of the guys on my team realize that they have those expectations of me. Sometimes it's annoying, but sometimes it's just funny."

"What about as an investigator? Is it just as hard?"

"Less so. There've been enough women in law enforcement over the years to remove some of the stigma. On the investigation side, I've run into very little sexism. It's when we get to the force reaction stuff that I start to run into it again. It's even weirder because while I'm getting the training, I know where I'm going to be slotted in the team—not as rapid force reaction but as an investigator."

"But they still make you take the training."

"Of course. I might be needed."

She caught his nod from the corner of her eye as the moonlight returned when a cloud moved on.

He startled her by holding out his hand. After a moment, she pulled her own hand from her pocket and returned his grip.

"I guess I know my weakness," he said, sounding faintly amused.

"What's that?"

"I like my mares strong."

For an instant she almost bridled, then she caught the humor and laughed. He squeezed her hand and she squeezed back. "You'll get sick of me soon enough," she promised.

"Only if you stick around long enough for me to find out."

What did he mean by that? All of a sudden her heart was galloping, and the air seemed to have been sucked out of the night. Then he turned to look at her. She wished there was more light, because she couldn't read his face.

"We're adults," he said. "I don't know about you, but I hate playing teenage games."

She managed a nod, but still couldn't speak.

"When a stallion wants a mare, he noses around until she gives him an answer. The women decide, you know. Men ask, but women decide."

"Yes." The word came out on a mere whisper.

He tugged her hand. She rose, letting him draw her across the couple of feet that separated them. When he pulled her down on his lap, she offered no protest at all.

With her legs across the arm of the chair, and his arm around her back, she felt cradled in heat.

"It's cold out here," he said. "A good deterrent to keep us from going too far. I don't know about you, but I'd like to try a bit of this feeling on for size."

"Are…are you sure?"

"Aren't you? Aren't you curious about what you're feeling, what I'm feeling?"

"Yes. But…" But what? Now more than her heart was pounding. Her entire body had begun to throb with hunger. She wanted this man. Who cared what price there might be later? She'd paid it before, she could pay it again.

And the admission price, right now, didn't seem steep at all.

He moved his face closer, then waited. She turned a little toward him, and he closed the distance, his mouth finding hers surely. His hand came up to cup her cheek, warming it while his other arm continued to support her back.

She wasn't trapped. She could pull away, slide away, at any instant. But heavens, she didn't want to. She had the memory of a hug, of one kiss, and both of them goaded her to find out more about what this man could evoke in her.

Expectation and anticipation knotted in her as she opened herself to his kiss. Sometimes you just had to damn the consequences and push on because you knew if you didn't you'd regret it. Hell, that's what had gotten her out here in the first place.

And if she stopped this, she would wonder till her dying day what it might have been like with Dom.

That was not a question she wanted to leave unanswered.

Dom knew he was playing with fire, but something inside him was telling him it was time to come out of his cave. The cave where he'd been living since Mary's death, the safe little world where upsets were few and far between, and the risks of loss were minimized. Where he controlled as much as any human could.

Control had become very important to him. Too important. Some of that was good, because he had two boys to raise and protect. Some of it was unhealthy, because he'd circumscribed his life to this ranch, to his sons, to Mary's parents and people he couldn't avoid running into.

And in his drive to control everything he could control, he'd buried himself too deep in his work. He had filled every possible moment with chores around the ranch and taking care of the boys, but he'd forgotten to leave some room for himself.

All because he didn't want to risk the pain again.

But now something was pushing at him to take a first step, to make a new connection. He knew it wouldn't last, but he needed to take the step anyway.

Holding a woman again felt so good. Just the weight of her on his lap, the feel of her body against his, the way her mouth felt so soft and warm, those things tore down barriers he hadn't really been aware of.

Human contact. Not the kind he had with his kids, but the kind he'd been denying himself for a long time now.

When she slipped her arm up around his neck, he felt pure pleasure, pure welcome, of a kind that had long been gone from his life. And he realized just how much he missed it and needed it.

As if he'd been only half-alive for too long now.

He deepened his kiss and she welcomed him into the hot depths of her mouth. Tongues played tentatively at first, then with greater purpose and complete surety. Heat made his groin feel heavy, a delicious heat he'd been denied for too long.

Questions evaporated. The world went away.

Encouraged, he slid his hand from her cheek to her neck, and then lower to cup her breast. It was fuller than he expected, and the sensation of holding it, gently kneading it, quickened his heartbeat. Beneath his palm, through all the layers, he could feel her nipple harden in response.

Man, it was like stepping into warm sunshine after an

endless night. Nerves he had nearly forgotten sang with hope and need. Life reawakened in him, reminding him of all the goodness he'd been missing.

He wanted her, and for the first time in ages he remembered that wanting could be a good thing. Impulses long forgotten tore through him, filling him, and he was about to slide her from his lap so that he could embrace her more fully, discover her more fully, when somewhere in the dim recesses of his mind he heard an approaching car engine.

Tearing his mouth from Courtney's, ignoring her murmured protest, he looked up. Someone was coming up the long drive.

"Dom…"

Oh, the sweet sound of a woman's voice filled with longing. "Courtney…someone's coming."

She looked adorably confused for a couple of seconds, then leaped from his lap as if ejected by a spring. "What?"

"Someone's coming up the drive."

She turned and looked. "Great timing," she said a bit sharply.

He laughed. "Yeah. But damn, that was great."

He caught her hand and squeezed it quickly before releasing it. He didn't ask her how she felt about it. She had already let him know.

She sagged onto the chair beside him, and he was surprised to realize that she was suddenly feeling a bit shy. That seemed so out of character for her, from what he'd seen of her, but she seemed unwilling to look in his direction.

"Are you okay?" he asked.

"I usually require a couple of dinner dates before I go that far."

A laugh escaped him. "Having me cook for you doesn't count?"

At that she finally laughed a little herself and looked his

way. "I guess it does, cowboy. I guess it does." Then, "Who do you suppose is coming?"

"I have no idea. If someone called to let me know, I must have missed it."

"I probably could have missed anything short of a nuclear bomb in the last five minutes."

That made him feel good. "Me, too." In fact, the ache in his body didn't want to subside. And that felt good, too.

The car drew close enough that Dom could make out the shape of a sheriff's SUV with roof lights. "What the hell?" he wondered, standing.

"A sheriff?" Courtney asked, and he realized she had come to stand beside him. "Isn't this a little extreme because you didn't go to the feed store?"

"Yeah, except everybody around here knows everybody's business. I just hope something bad didn't happen." His first thought, of course, was Mary's parents. His stomach did an uncomfortable flip.

The SUV pulled to a stop near the porch, and Gage Dalton climbed out, his scarred face shadowed from the moon by the brim of his tan Stetson, but otherwise familiar in his lean ranginess and the way he limped.

"Evening, Dom," Gage said.

"Is something wrong?"

"Not a thing. Just thought I'd stop by."

Dom leaned forward, putting both hands on the railing. "You guys drive up without warning, and I leap to awful conclusions."

"Sorry. It was an impulse as I was passing on the way home. I was out looking in on the Kipes."

Gage stepped onto the porch and Dom made introductions. "Sheriff Gage Dalton, Agent Courtney Tyson."

"Micah told me about you," Gage said as he shook Courtney's hand. "So you think Mary was murdered?"

"It's a possibility."

Dalton nodded. Then he turned to Dom. "Sorry, didn't mean to worry you, but I was just about to pass your place when I remembered what Micah said."

Courtney spoke. "Is it all over the state now?"

"Micah wouldn't tell anyone but me," Gage said with certainty. "I just thought I'd check in since I was practically on your doorstep."

"Come on in," Dom said. "I can make some coffee."

"That'd be nice," Gage agreed. "Thanks. I'd love a decent cup. My stomach's getting too cranky to handle Velma's brew anymore."

"Velma?" Courtney asked as they walked to the kitchen. She almost gasped as the light revealed the burn scars on one side of Gage's face that had before been hidden by shadows. She caught herself just in time.

"Our dispatcher," Gage said, removing his hat and hanging it on the back of an empty chair. "You could use her coffee for battery acid but nobody has the heart to tell her. I didn't mind so much ten years ago."

"Velma's an institution," Dom agreed as he started the coffeepot. "Not a lady you want on your wrong side."

Gage grinned lopsidedly as he sat, and looked at Courtney. "Velma seems to have been dispatcher since Moses was a boy. I don't think anyone's gonna ever pry her from that desk. And she's mother hen to damn near the entire county. I think we'd have an uprising if we ever tried to retire her."

"She's been there my entire life," Dom said. He joined them at the table while the coffee brewed. "So what prompted this impulse of yours?"

"I told you. I heard Agent Tyson thinks Mary was murdered."

Dom settled back. "And?"

"And," Gage said, "I wanted to know if there's anything we can do to help locally."

Courtney felt astonished. No one had offered her any help on this case after the first few weeks. "This is unofficial," she said finally.

"I know. Micah told me. You met the stone wall."

"Exactly. So I don't want it getting out anywhere that I'm looking into it."

"It might surprise you," Gage said, "given that I'm here because of what Micah told me, but we can be the soul of discretion in the department. People in this county trust us not to gossip. If it doesn't make the logs or the prosecutor's office, it doesn't get out. Loose lips are frowned on."

"But obviously you talk among yourselves."

Gage gave his lopsided smile. "But only among ourselves, and only when it's necessary. Micah thought maybe we could help in some way. Mary was one of ours. So consider our resources at your disposal if you need them. And if you need us to look into things without letting anyone know why, or who we're helping, that's entirely possible."

"Thank you." For some odd reason her eyes started to burn. "You don't know…" She couldn't even think how to phrase what she was feeling.

"I know. I was DEA before I came here. Resource allocation can be infuriating. I've been faced with someone higher-up deciding a case was too iffy and the cost not worth it."

She nodded.

"It leaves you feeling very alone and very angry," Gage said. "So, you're not alone now if you need some help. I've got sources that reach far outside this county, and every one of them is discreet."

"I can't thank you enough."

"It's the kind of thing I can't ignore, Ms. Tyson. I'm just not built that way."

"Me, either," she admitted.

Dom noticed she glanced his way, as if still unsure what he thought about this. His feelings hadn't changed—in the end it didn't really matter how Mary had died—but faced with two people who believed that was an issue, he wasn't about to trot out his contrariness.

But depending on how things went over the next few days, he might trot it out for Courtney again. Because all of a sudden he needed her to understand something. Something important. And they'd have to sort it out somehow.

But for now he just nodded noncommittally and let the sheriff and the agent talk. Later there'd be time for other stuff.

Chapter 11

The conversation with Gage Dalton left Courtney feeling better. She didn't see how she could use his offer of help, at least not yet, but he had indeed made her feel less alone on her quest. More justified in making it.

Dom hadn't really looked thrilled, but he hadn't objected. He also hadn't made another pass at her, but after Gage left it was getting late and she'd thought it politic to go to bed.

Just why, she wasn't sure, especially since she wound up lying awake and staring into the dark for hours. She heard him come upstairs, heard him close his bedroom door for the night.

And then all alone in the dark, she tried to ask herself what the hell she was doing. There weren't any answers, not anymore.

Just questions. Too many questions.

Nor did they get answered over the next days. She found herself falling easily into the rhythms of the ranch. The boys seemed to like her and she wound up doing all sorts of things with them, from chores, to schoolwork, to just playing hide-and-seek.

She finished going through the things in "Mary's Box" as she'd come to think of the large filing box Dom had given her, and she'd found nothing else.

She had no case. No case at all.

Well, she told herself, it had all been worth it just to meet Mary's family. Dom had apparently put whatever had begun to brew between them on a back burner, because he didn't approach her again. Just as well, she told herself.

Guilt still plagued her a bit, as if she were illicitly attracted to her friend's husband, even though she knew Mary's death had changed all that. What's more, she was leaving soon, going back to Georgia, and both of them knew they didn't want to live that way. He'd been through it once. She didn't want to try it.

So the most they could have was a fling. And maybe they'd both be happier in the end if they didn't.

She even expected him to call off their trip to watch the migrations, but he didn't. Indeed, Friday afternoon he packed a duffel for the boys and took them to their grandparents' house.

Left alone, she accessed her private email folder and scanned once again the case notes she had taken, the evidence that she had managed to make copies of. And for the hundredth time, she tried to put it all together in a way that would reveal something other than what she already knew:

Some Iraqi women and girls had been raped, most likely by troops. They didn't even know how many. The Iraqi women wouldn't talk, many of their husbands and fathers didn't want to see them shamed if even they knew about it, and the few who had gotten mad enough to complain didn't know enough to make a complete case.

Mary had gotten wind of it, though. After Courtney had asked her to keep her ear to the ground, apparently she managed to ask a few questions, just enough to let Courtney know that the rapes had occurred.

Between cultural attitudes toward rape and the high wall of distrust between the occupiers and the locals, no one wanted to say anything.

But apparently Mary had become enough of a threat that they'd killed her. Because the result of the roadside attack that had killed Mary simply didn't fit an insurgent attack. Only one person dead? No one else injured? And only one vehicle in the convoy, contrary to operational orders. There should have been another Humvee in addition to the one carrying Mary and the two corpsmen who took care of male patients at the clinic. At least one, pacified zone or not.

Yes, she thought, putting her head in her hand. It could just be an amazing confluence of factors. But since she had been slated to meet Mary only two days later, since Mary had let her know she had learned something, Courtney found it hard to believe that this all had been random chance.

Then she heard a ping and looked up at her email. Her friend had answered, with pointed brevity.

"Captain Anderson D. Metcalfe."

Courtney froze, and a moment later her stomach plummeted. She knew that name. Captain Metcalfe was an academy graduate, the son of an army general with tons of power and pull. No doubt Captain Metcalfe was destined for great things.

No doubt if he was in any way involved in what had happened either to the Iraqi women or Mary, he was untouchable. Courtney had requested background info from Lena if she found a face match and its absence from the email spoke volumes. Large volumes. It was hands-off, and stand down.

She swore quietly and put her head back in her hands. That was it. Dead end. Her superiors had been correct: she was wasting time and resources.

Because some people couldn't be touched. A word in the right ear, and unless someone had an ironclad case with a dozen witnesses and video and paper to back it up, the case would be dismissed.

She didn't have anywhere near that.

Her hand was played out, and no matter how she despaired, no matter how much the bile rose in her throat, she began to accept that there would be no justice for Mary or those rape victims. None. Not even a day in court.

Swearing again, under her breath, she switched off the computer. Brick walls at every turn. It made her feel no better…in fact it made her feel angrier…to think those bricks might have been deliberately placed in her path.

But she'd also been around the block enough times to know that this was a battle she couldn't win. If she beat her head on that wall enough, she'd merely come away bloodied and probably out of a job, with nothing at all accomplished.

For an instant she felt an uncharacteristic urge to smash something, but she fought the impulse. Smashing something would fix nothing, and merely leave something broken. She'd learned that years ago when her dad had died.

"Courtney? Are you okay?"

She started and looked around to discover Dom had returned. "Yes. No. I don't know."

He came into the room and sat facing her. For an instant she thought he was going to reach out and take her hand, but with almost visible effort he refrained. "What happened?"

"That guy whose photo I sent to my friend?"

"Yeah?"

"He's a general's son."

"Oh."

"Untouchable," she said, in case he hadn't gotten it.

"That's probably why he looked familiar to you, then."

"Maybe."

"So you've reached a dead end."

"Evidently."

He leaned back in his chair, frowning faintly, studying her. "That's okay."

"Okay? How can it possibly be okay?" Her voice had risen, and she caught herself with effort. "Why should he get off? Just because his dad is powerful?"

"Do you have any proof that he did any of this?"

"Not enough."

"Well, then. That's it. And somehow you've got to let go of it."

"How can you say that? It was your wife!"

For an instant he didn't move except to tighten his mouth into a stern line. God, she hated to see that, especially when she knew how soft and generous that mouth could be. *Stop it,* she told herself. It was better this way. Let him be angry with her. It would make it easier for her to leave.

Then he rose. "Come with me. I want you to see something."

Feeling as if every muscle in her body dragged, she followed him into the living room. He walked over to a shelf and pointed to a triangular case containing a U.S. flag and beside it another case containing a Purple Heart, a combat theater medal and a good conduct medal, plus Mary's medical, unit and rank insignia.

"You see that?"

She nodded. He stared at them for a few seconds, then faced her. "My boys have that. It's not much, but it tells them their mother was a hero who died in the service of her country."

"She did!"

"Exactly. They've accepted she was a soldier, a casualty of war. Now you tell me just what good it will do for them to be told their mother was murdered by one of her fellow soldiers. You tell me how that will make them one bit happier, or make their loss one bit easier to bear. You tell me how that won't make them bitter or angry."

Courtney caught her breath. "That's why you can live without justice?"

"What the hell good will justice do except damage those boys? People die. I watch animals all the time, and the amazing thing is they don't seem to be hung up on justice. They accept that the weak or young will fall. It's the natural order. That doesn't mean it doesn't hurt, but tell me, Courtney, just what you think *justice* is going to fix. It's not going to bring Mary back. It's not going to erase the violation of those Iraqi women. It's not going to fix a damn thing. War is an atrocity-making situation."

"But..."

"No buts. I'm not saying this guy, or whoever it was, did the right thing, or that it was excusable. I'm not saying he doesn't deserve to pay the price for what he did. But I'm not keen on having my boys' life ripped up by the fact that their mother may have been killed by people she should have been able to trust. That's a lesson they're too young to learn."

He hesitated then added, "Justice won't bring your dad back, either. It may not even provide as much satisfaction as you think."

He left her standing there, shaken to the core.

An hour later she discovered he was still planning for them to head up into the mountains to watch the migration. She went into the kitchen and found him with the saddlebags again, stuffing things into the panniers.

She expressed her surprise. "We're still going?"

"Why wouldn't we be?" He smiled at her.

"I thought…I thought…"

"That I was mad at you? I'm not in the least. I was just explaining my viewpoint. Now, do you want to go? If so, get your things."

Yes, she wanted to go. Even after the shakeup he'd just given her, she very much wanted to go. But as she bundled up clothes to take with her, she did something she hadn't done since her arrival: she tucked her service weapon into her belt holster, and hid it beneath a baggy sweatshirt.

That may have indeed been a careless hunter last weekend, but she couldn't forget it. Especially now that she knew who had been the subject of her inquiry. Since opening that email this afternoon, she'd had a paranoid thought: that she was up against some shadowy cabal, the same cabal that had killed Mary. That her request for a face match may have come to someone's attention.

Man! She sat on the edge of her bed, wondering if this trip was wise. Just suppose someone was coming after her. She'd be exposing Dom, too. And her safety this past week on the ranch might owe entirely to the fact that if she got shot right around here, no one would be able to blame it on a hunting accident.

But up in the woods and mountains, the story changed.

She shook her head, telling herself she was in danger of building a mountain out of a molehill. Of course she was. Her friend was discreet. For anyone but her friend to have learned about the query on the face recognition software, someone would have had to have Metcalfe's file flagged.

Of course, someone who was the son of a prominent general, someone destined for the highest corridors of military power himself, might be able to arrange such a thing. Might.

Careers of this sort were protected, ranks closed, people cooperated in hopes of advancing their own careers.

It wouldn't be the first time she'd run into a brick wall, but it would be the first time she might have to quit.

She touched the bulge under her sweatshirt, and decided that yes, she was definitely taking it with her. One single shot in the woods meant nothing, usually. People hunted all the time where and when they weren't supposed to. And of course, no one was supposed to know where she was. But just in case....

Decision made, she scooped up her clothes and toiletries and headed downstairs. "Are we taking a packhorse again?" she asked Dom as he began stuffing her things into a second set of saddlebags.

"Depends. You mind roughing it? It's supposed to be clear tonight, so we don't even need a tent. But there's also an old line shack we can use. Not nearly as nice as the cabin where we stayed last week, but adequate shelter."

"That's fine by me."

He looked up, smiling faintly. "I imagine you've had some training in roughing it."

"You could say so. Although I like it better here than some of the places I've had to camp out. I'll take the chill over the heat any day."

"No mosquitoes, either, not now. Been too dry and cold."

"I'll vote for that, too. Do you get a lot of mosquitoes?"

"In the spring and early summer usually. The run-off pools, the ground gets soggy in places, and yeah, we have lots of mosquitoes for a while. That's part of the reason I'm glad I can take the horses to higher pastures. The higher we go, the fewer the insects."

"Maybe I ought to just camp out there all summer. I hate mosquitoes."

He chuckled. "I can always use somebody to keep an eye on my stock."

"Yeah, I'd be really good at that." She passed him a couple of rolled-up T-shirts from her stack.

"You probably would be. Think of all the peace and quiet. Nights under starry skies. No bad guys."

"An occasional mountain lion. A coyote. A wolf."

He laughed. "That's always possible, although they tend to stay away when they smell people."

"I'd sure be ripe after a few days."

"What? No bathing in icy mountain streams?"

"I'd rather drink from one."

He shook his head, his smile fading as he stuffed the last of her things into the saddlebag. "Don't do that. The days of safe mountain water are long gone."

"How come?"

"Too many people and too many beavers. They've carried some pretty nasty bugs up those streams. It's almost impossible nowadays to find one it's safe to drink from."

"That's sad. But it doesn't make the horses sick?"

"Nope. But I still treat them for it anyway when I bring them back down. I don't want the kids picking it up. And they could, which is why you won't see them shoveling manure very often. Not until I'm sure they get the whole hand-washing thing down."

"They're young yet," she agreed.

"And forgetful. It's always that one slip that gets you."

"Don't I know it."

By the time they were ready to go, the sun had already disappeared behind the western peaks, although the day remained pretty bright.

"Do we have time?"

"Sure. It's not that far by the direct route."

They took an entirely different path from last weekend, a

steeper one, but much more open. She didn't meet many of the thrilling views this time, although once they rode along an extensive gorge where water raced so rapidly that it drowned out every other sound.

Just as the light reached that vision-deadening point between day and night, when everything seemed to flatten, they emerged in a small glade. Here and there a few late flowers bloomed in brilliant color, almost like tiny little fairy lights, even though the deciduous trees around them had shed almost the last of their leaves. Conifers rose tall and proud, seeming to tickle the sky with their tips, turning black as the light faded. Against one forest wall stood an old shack, barely bigger than the average suburban storage shed.

After they dismounted, she noted that Dom merely loosened the cinches on the saddles, but didn't remove them. "Are you going to leave them saddled all night?"

"They actually don't mind. They're workhorses. As long as I give them room to breathe, they're happy. I wouldn't do this more than a night or two at most, though." He hobbled them, removed the saddlebags, then let them wander around grazing and drinking from a nearby stream.

On the grass he spread a canvas tarp, then opened two sleeping bags on it. "See, we can sit out here for a while and enjoy the evening. We don't even have to use the shack unless you want."

Given the gunshot that insisted on ringing in her memory, she thought the shack might be the better option for later. She sat cross-legged on the sleeping bag he pointed to, and watched night engulf the world. "This is incredible."

"You don't spend a lot of nights outdoors? I'd have thought you would, given what you do now."

"Not without six to ten other guys." She shook her head. "Sometimes they're quiet because we're on an operation. Other times they'd scare off any wildlife within forty miles. But at no time do we just sit and enjoy nightfall. And even so, most of our operational training isn't for woodland settings."

"That's a shame."

At that moment she would have agreed with him. It was fascinating to watch the light seep away and darkness creep in. In a matter of minutes, the whole world seemed to change. Now, when she tipped her head back, she could see the millions of stars overhead, so many she couldn't imagine being able to count them. "God, I'd forgotten it could be so peaceful!"

"It's easy to forget everything out here."

"Is that why you like it?"

"That's only part of the reason. I just like being surrounded by nature. I always have."

She leaned back until her head rested on the sleeping bag and she stared up. "I could get addicted to this."

"I already am."

She felt him reach out and curl his fingers around hers. She managed not to stiffen, but realized that if he went any farther, he was going to discover the gun clipped to her belt. Trying to move slowly, she reached for it and silently unclipped it, then tucked it under her sleeping bag.

She didn't know why she felt she had to conceal it. He'd ridden up here, after all, with a shotgun holstered on his saddle, and she'd seen his gun cabinet. And just a few minutes ago, after laying out the sleeping bags, he put his shotgun on the tarp within reach. This wasn't a man with a moral objection to guns.

Maybe it was because the years had taught her that most men felt uncomfortable with a woman who wore a sidearm most of the time.

Regardless, it was done, and for now she gave herself up to the exquisite feeling of his large hand wrapped around hers.

"So you used to fall asleep dreaming about falling into the stars?" he murmured.

"Yeah. Do you ever feel when you're lying down like this that you're almost weightless and you could just fall upward right into them?"

"Sometimes. Mostly when I was kid. I used to wish I could be an astronaut."

She smiled, even though he couldn't see it. "Yeah, I played with that idea for a while, too. What changed your mind?"

"The horses. I couldn't bring myself to leave them behind."

"You really *are* attached."

"Completely."

She wondered if that was some kind of warning. Even if it wasn't she should probably take it that way. Anyone who wanted this man would be tied to his ranch, to his way of life. And considering the grief and anger he'd felt toward Mary for her long absences, did she really want to put him in that position again?

Not that things had gotten that far between them. But it was good to think of all the dangers before you got in over your head. And it would be easy to get in over her head with Dom. That much was clear.

Time to think of something else, she warned herself. "Are we likely to see any elk or stuff in the morning?"

"If we get up very early, and we're very quiet, there's a pretty good chance. I've watched this migration for years. You're not apt to see huge herds. This isn't going to be like the African savannah. But we should see at least a few elk or pronghorns. Maybe a family group if we're lucky."

"And if we're not?"

"Then we'll have gotten up early and enjoyed a gorgeous sunrise."

"Works for me." She smiled again and squeezed his hand.

The night air was cooling rapidly, but that wasn't unusual at higher elevations where the air was thinner and the sun slipped behind mountains long before official sunset. "I'm glad we can't build a fire."

"Why's that?"

"Because then I wouldn't be able to see anything but the fire."

A quiet chuckle escaped him.

Somewhere an owl hooted, a lonely, beautiful sound. "So there are wolves around here?"

"We've got a pack or two in these mountains."

"Do they follow the migration?"

"Not exactly. They take advantage of it, of course, but wolves are pretty territorial. They have a certain range they stick to, and seldom venture beyond it. And now with all the packs in Yellowstone, they're even more territorial and cautious."

"I read or heard somewhere that you can keep them away with a recording of their calls."

"Yeah, I heard that, too." He rolled on his side and propped himself on an elbow. Her eyesight had been steadily adapting, and even though the moon hadn't risen yet, she could see him clearly enough in the starshine. "I don't especially want to keep them away."

"Why not?"

"They're part of the ecology. They don't often bother my horses, they seem to prefer not to get into it with my dogs." He fell silent for a moment. "I've seen changes since they started roaming around here."

"Like what?"

"There seems to be more food. Some plants that had almost been grazed out by deer and elk have started to come back."

Courtney pondered for a few minutes. "I thought most ranchers hated wolves."

"Some do. But from what I've been reading, restoring the apex predator has been beneficial overall for the ecology. Sometimes you just have to make compromises, and realize that Mother Nature is going to take her due one way or another. My vote is for a healthy ecology."

"Which is why you opened some of your land for the migratory route."

"Exactly."

"But will hunters use those corridors?"

"It's private land. They're not supposed to. But yeah, I imagine some will. Limited licenses help."

"I think that's called herd management."

"Yeah." He laughed. "I don't object to hunting, as long as it takes into account that you don't want to cull the wild herds too much. The thing is, the herds are actually healthier now that wolves have come back. And there's less starvation in the winter, so they're even growing a bit."

"That's good."

"I think so." He scooted closer. Letting go of her hand, he reached out to lay his palm on her midriff. "Feeling adventurous?"

Warm tingles were already spreading from his touch. "I'm always up for adventure."

"Under the stars? With owls hooting?"

"And wolves prowling?"

"I'm the only wolf I hear in the area right now."

A deep happiness began to fill her. "Do they make noise when they're around?"

"That's how they keep in touch. But I may be the only one howling."

She lifted a hand and pressed it gently to his chest. "This past week…" She hesitated, uncertain how to say it.

"This past week I've been trying to avoid something I wasn't sure about."

"What are you sure of now?"

"That I want you. Of that I'm very sure."

Slowly, feeling at once shy and brave, she slid her hand up until she cupped his neck. "I'm pretty sure, too." Sure that she wanted an answer to all the questions he'd made her ask since the first time he'd kissed her. She wanted to know. It might all come to naught, in fact it probably would, but right now she didn't care. They had this night, and this night was one she wanted, even if she never knew another like it.

"Yes," she whispered, as if he'd asked a question.

He bent and kissed her, this time with little gentleness and a lot of demand. She reveled in the feeling, as if he were claiming her, rather than asking her. She opened her mouth, begging him inside her, and he obliged instantly, finding her tongue with his, filling her with a warmth in delicious contrast to the cooling air. Their tongues dueled, playing an ancient game of thrust and parry, promising ever so much more.

Pinwheels of fire began to sparkle behind her eyelids as if the very stars of heaven had descended to join them.

His hand slipped up beneath her sweatshirt, warm and rough against tender skin. Along with it came some chilly air, more delicious contrast, but one that made her shiver.

He drew back suddenly. "Wait," he said thickly.

Wait? She blinked as he lifted her from the sleeping bag and set her on the tarp. She heard zippers rattling, and realized he was going to put the sleeping bags together.

The thought excited her, but an instant later she remembered her weapon. Quickly she reached out and tucked it under the very edge of the tarp.

Even in the dark she could tell he moved swiftly. Was he afraid she would change her mind? Not likely. She could almost have laughed at the idea. But maybe he was as impatient as she was.

Remember this, she told herself. Remember every touch, every sensation, every single instant of this night, because it might never happen again. Somehow she knew it was going to be special, the kind of memory she'd want to take out and relive again and again. She had few enough of those.

"There." The bags were together, and he smoothed them out. Then kneeling, he faced her and began to pull off his clothes. Even though there was nothing but starlight yet, she could see enough to make her draw and hold her breath.

A smoothly muscled chest, not the kind that came from a gym, but the kind that came from hard work day in and out. Strong arms that had just lifted her easily.

Then he reached for his belt. On impulse, she rose to her knees and reached out for the buckle. It crossed her mind to wonder if she was being too pushy—a complaint she had often heard—but she shoved it aside. Unfastening a man's belt buckle was so erotic that she wanted to enjoy the freedom of doing it herself.

He didn't object. He simply moved a little to make it easier for her, and just then the first rays of the quarter moon found the glade, falling on him, silvering him in the pale light.

He was gorgeous.

She released the buckle, tugged at the snap. A breeze whispered overhead in the trees, a soft sighing that was not so very different from the sound that escaped her as he rose on his knees and pulled down his zipper.

When he reached to pull his pants down, she held her breath, watching. He was perfect. Magnificent. And wonderfully aroused. He pawed around in a pocket and brought out a condom. She took it from him and savored rolling it onto his staff, especially because he groaned as she did it.

When his jeans reached his knees, he turned and sat. "Boots," he said with something like disgust.

A happy little laugh escaped her and she crawled over to help him pull them off. Then his jeans joined the heap of his shirt and jacket.

He turned to her. She was so busy filling her eyes with his magnificence that she might have been a rag doll as he pulled her sweatshirt over her head. Her bra followed it onto the grass and she realized she'd never made love outdoors before. Never. The cool night air on her bare breasts aroused her.

The heat pooling between her legs grew abruptly heavier. The night wind in the trees kicked up, a rushing sound that seemed to reach inside her head as passion throbbed more strongly.

"You're beautiful," he said, his voice barely carrying above the wind. "I want to touch you. But I don't want you to get cold."

He reached for her jeans and she lay back immediately, allowing him to strip away the rest of her clothing and her boots. Then he lifted her a bit, his skin feeling cool now against hers and tucked her into the joined sleeping bags. Only a moment later he slid in beside her.

At once he pulled her into the curve of his body, at first snuggling with her while their body heat gradually filled the bags with warmth.

But as the warmth of the insulated air around them grew, so did the warmth deep inside her. Skin against skin felt so startlingly good to her that she wondered if she'd ever noticed it before, or if she'd simply forgotten.

Slowly his hands began to rub her back, warming her more, and with each movement drawing her closer and closer to him until they were pressed together from head to foot.

"You feel good," he murmured in her ear. "You feel good all over."

"So do you." Her hands wandered over him now, too, finding angles and planes and hollows. Very little of him seemed soft or yielding, not even his rump.

"You have the hardest butt," she murmured, and giggled.

"It's all that riding. But yours isn't exactly a pillow," he said as he ran his hands over her, making her shiver.

"It's all that jogging."

He laughed, then swooped in for a deep kiss, while his hands painted fire all over her. He found her breast, teasing her nipple until it was hard and aching then followed with his mouth, sucking on her until she felt it all the way through her body.

At some point, she lost track of everything: the night, the chill, the owl that hooted forlornly, the wind that was building in the trees. She suddenly straddled him, with no memory of making the decision to do so, and she felt his manhood sandwiched between them, as hard and strong as he.

He didn't seem to mind at all. He simply gripped her hips and held her there. "You're driving me nuts," he muttered huskily.

"That makes…two of us…" Oh, man, she was losing it, losing it, and she wasn't even moving, but she was going to go right over the edge just like this, impossibly.

Then his hands lifted her and lowered her swiftly. In that instant he filled her, claimed her, owned her.

For the first time in her life, she didn't mind feeling possessed. She gloried in it. Tipping her head back a little, even as she rested her hands on his shoulders, she caught sight of the stars. They beckoned to her, almost calling her name.

Then he moved. A shock wave of desire passed through her, riveting her on a pillar of need. She moved, too, and after a few seconds they found their rhythm together.

Like riding a horse, she thought hazily. Or a rocket to the stars.

She heard him groan, and the sound fueled her own need. When he heaved up at her, she pressed down until he couldn't get any farther inside her.

Again. Again. The stars seemed to come closer, and she couldn't tell if they were falling or she was rising. Then her eyes closed as passion took her fully in its grip.

The ache grew, goading, nearly painful, until at last she went supernova. The explosion inside her head was almost as big as the one in her body.

Shuddering with powerful aftershocks, she sank down on Dom and felt him wrap her in a strong embrace, holding her snugly as if he felt they might fly apart.

Life was so damn good sometimes.

Chapter 12

"It's time."

A quiet murmur caused her to open one heavy-lidded eye. Dom leaned over her, barely visible in the setting moon's light. "Already?" Her voice cracked. She ached deliciously from head to foot, and vaguely remembered having tried a few things last night that she'd never tried before.

Instant heat pooled between her legs. She could think of lots of things she'd rather do than go look for elk.

"We can skip it," he said, sounding amused. "I'm not opposed to staying right here."

Before she could answer, he kissed her. It was the kiss of a lover sure of his welcome, sure he had pleased his lady. She liked it.

She also would have liked more of it, but her stomach chose that moment to growl loudly.

Dom chuckled. "I think we need to tend to some other needs first."

Reluctantly she agreed. A noisy stomach, especially one as noisy as hers was being, would ruin the atmosphere.

He helped her dress swiftly; it had grown almost bitterly cold, and emerging from the sleeping bag was a test of willpower. Her clothes felt chilly and damp, but she knew from experience they would heat up soon enough.

"I'm going to make a fire in the shack," he said. "Just enough to make some coffee and heat some food."

"Okay. I'll be there in a second. Nature calls."

"Nature has a way of doing that."

As soon as Dom disappeared into the line shack, she clipped her weapon to her belt again and headed for the trees to take care of business.

A few minutes later, she was inside with him. He slipped an arm around her as they watched the logs on a small and very old Franklin stove begin to burn brightly.

"I believe," Dom said, "that every morning, however early, must begin with hot coffee."

"It sure helps. I consider it a fine luxury."

He turned and dropped a kiss on her lips. "You look beautiful for a lady who tumbled around in the metaphoric hay most of the night."

She felt a smile tip the corners of her mouth. "Maybe that's what made me beautiful."

"Ah, I get the credit. Very nice of you considering you're a born wildcat." He winked then released her as he poked at the logs. "Nice dry wood. Coffee won't be long."

She leaned back against a very small, very rickety table and watched him work with an old-fashioned metal pot, putting grounds from a pouch in the basket, and pouring in some bottled water. It wasn't long before the wonderful aroma of brewing coffee filled the small space.

"In case you're wondering," he said, "we're not eating food bars for breakfast."

"No?"

"I'm better than that."

Apparently so, because he managed to turn some powdered eggs, a handful of bacon bits and some slivers of hard cheese into a wonderful omelet served on blue-and-white spattered metal plates. The forks looked almost as old as the cabin, but they worked. As for the coffee, while she usually preferred hers made by the drip method, unless she could get espresso, she was sure she'd never tasted a better cup of brew than what she drank from that metal cup.

"Want to hear about one of the guys I'm training with?" she asked as they ate.

"Sure."

"He brings a French press coffeemaker with him on our exercises. Always."

Dom cocked a brow. "They let him?"

"Believe it or not. He has one that's metal, and he packs it in with his clothes. If we light fires, his is the most popular one around."

"I can imagine." He glanced toward the battered old pot on the Franklin stove. "Maybe I should get one of those."

"I'm not complaining. This coffee is fabulous."

"It's the early hour and the company," he said, winking.

They left the dishes for later, because he expressed concern that the hour was getting late.

It didn't feel late to Courtney. It was pitch-dark when they went back outside. The horses shuffled over to them, as if knowing immediately that it was time to work.

Courtney rolled up the sleeping bags and folded the tarp, taking them into the shack while Dom tended the horses. By the time she returned outside, they were ready. She mounted easily, finding the movements familiar now, and Marti followed comfortably behind Dom's mount.

She could definitely get used to this. The danger of that

thought hit her hard almost immediately. She couldn't afford to get used to this. She was leaving. Monday morning at the latest. She was going to leave all of this behind because on every level except the irrational, she knew it wouldn't work. She couldn't be Mary's substitute, and Dom had already been clear about how much trouble he'd had accepting that his wife was away more often than not.

She'd be just another version of the same. He didn't want that. No way. Her heart plummeted, and her mind argued with it. No time to be stupid. Just watch the migration, enjoy the weekend, and tuck it away like a delicious vacation, a memory and nothing else.

They climbed high into the woods, Dom and his mount Arnett finding their way despite the darkness. She couldn't see all that much since the forest had closed in around them, but Marti moved sure-footedly. Courtney heard the rushing of water from time to time, but it didn't seem very close. The breeze still blew through the treetops and occasionally found a path to reach down and buffet her, too.

Nearly an hour passed and Courtney thought she could sense just the slightest change in the sky overhead. Not exactly a lightening, but somehow the stars seemed not quite as bright. Dawn must be near.

Dom called a halt at last, and Marti quite naturally edged her way up beside him.

"We'll leave the horses here. I don't want them to scare the herds."

"Won't we do that?"

"We'll try to stay downwind. That should be easy this morning. But at least I can trust you not to whinny."

She almost laughed. "Are you sure of that?"

"After last night, there's a whole lot I'm not so sure about anymore."

With that enigmatic remark, he swung to the ground. She

wanted to ask what he meant, but decided this might be a bad time. Worse, she wasn't sure she wanted to hear his answers, all of which probably included some version of saying goodbye soon. The inevitable was approaching, and her mood sank. She had to make a really strong effort to remind herself they were here to enjoy the migration. The rest was just a fantasy to be enjoyed briefly.

Once the horses were tethered, their cinches loosened, they continued the trip on foot. The sky *had* lightened just a bit. Courtney could see just enough not to fall flat on her face as they followed what she decided must be a mountain goat track, because surely it hadn't been beaten here by human feet. It was rugged, requiring them to grab onto rocks and trees as they clambered up.

Suddenly Dom stopped. He turned and held a finger to his lips. She nodded.

A few more steps and they were in deep grass, off the trail, hemmed in by trees. But even from here she could see a more open space ahead of them.

Dom pointed to it. "They usually come through over there. Let's settle here."

"Why there? They don't want to hide in the trees?"

"They're not worried about hiding. But we had a fire up here about seven years ago, and it turned this area into some really good grazing."

He bent back some of the grass so that they could see the open area, then they sat on the ground, waiting.

"I should have brought the tarp," he whispered. "You'll get a cold bottom."

"Then you can warm it up."

The grin he flashed her was huge.

A pinkish glow began to permeate the sky and she felt Dom stiffen.

"What?" she whispered.

"Shh. Listen."

She strained her ears and then she heard it. It was almost a snuffling sound, followed by some crunching. She held her breath, feeling she was about to experience magic.

And moments later she did. No elk but instead what she assumed was a pronghorn, a deer, smaller than she expected. He sported horns that split near the top, one portion pointing backward, the other forward. At once she understood why they were called pronghorns. But then she indentified them by another name. She was looking at an antelope.

He was chewing on something as he surveyed the clearing. He made an odd noise, sounding every bit as ugly as a crow's caw, then stepped forward. Behind him came a few does, also with two-pronged horns and then a bunch of youngsters about half his size.

A whole family. She felt her heart leap, and she drew a deep, quiet breath, not wanting to startle them.

The herd spread out, eating noisily of grass and sometimes pulling leaves off bushes. But they never stopped moving for long. Always, always they edged toward the far end of the clearing, eating as they went.

God, she wished she had her camera. As the day brightened, she could see more of their reddish color, and the brilliant white patches on their throats.

Suddenly they all froze and lifted their heads, looking upslope. A moment later one of them gave that ugly cry again, and they took off. Fast. Faster than she would have believed possible. In an instant they were gone.

"What scared them?" she asked quietly.

"I don't know. Maybe they got wind of us. Maybe they smelled or heard a cat approach."

"Cat?"

"Bobcat. Not that one could catch them." He smiled,

his eyes crinkling in the corners. "They're the fastest land mammals, second only to cheetahs. Pretty amazing, huh?"

"Fantastic. One eyeblink and they were gone. And to think I wasn't all that excited about seeing pronghorns."

He laughed almost silently. "Did you want an elk?"

"Or a moose."

"We can hang out here for a while. There's no telling what might come along."

She was more than glad to do exactly that, especially when he put his arm around her and hugged her to his side.

She couldn't think of a better way to spend the morning.

They saw another, smaller herd of pronghorn before Dom judged it time to leave. "We can come back up this evening or in the morning, if you like. Or we can just go back to the house."

She thought about that as they walked back to the horses. She enjoyed being totally alone out here with Dom, but she enjoyed the ranch, too. Except at the ranch there would be inevitable distractions. The thought that Dom could ignore his horses, their needs and their training if they were nearby struck her as unlikely at best.

She wanted him all to herself for another day, however selfish that might be. Another day to see him smile, to talk about nothing of importance, to give in to the desire that seemed to steam between them even now as they walked through the woods. Somehow she was certain it wouldn't be quite as easy back at his ranch, even though the boys were at their grandparents.

Returning there would remind her of how soon she needed to leave.

"I'd like to stay," she said honestly. But even as she said it, another thought surprised her. "I miss Kyle and Todd!"

"I do, too. But this is their weekend to have fun and forget the ranch."

She turned to look at him. "Then let's make it that kind of weekend for you, too."

A smile lit his face. "You got it, lady." He gave her bottom a playful swat and she squeaked.

"I'm not one of your horses," she said with mock severity.

"Ah, but it's such a pleasure to ride you!"

Her cheeks burned instantly. But another fire, one that had only been banked by last night, was flaring, too. Evidently he saw it in her face, because his eyes darkened.

It was a race to get back to the line shack.

During the late afternoon, clouds moved in and the weather turned unexpectedly chilly. They cuddled around the Franklin stove, drinking coffee and eating canned soup and crackers.

"It was supposed to be clear all weekend," Dom remarked. "I guess this should blow through quickly."

Courtney listened to wind whistle through chinks in the cabin. "What about the horses?"

"You're beginning to sound ranch-bred." He smiled. "They'll be fine. They'll find a protected spot in the trees."

He had unsaddled them this time and brought the saddles and tack inside where the saddles now made decent, if hard, pillows. The saddle blankets themselves were coarse, and not the kind of thing she wanted against her skin.

Of course, tucked into the sleeping bag as she was, the only thing she was wearing was her sweatshirt to keep her shoulders warm.

"Did you ever hear that old joke?" she asked him. "About the lady who wanted the hem of all her nightgowns edged with fur?"

"Sounds familiar, but I'm not sure."

"Well, her dressmaker asked her why she wanted the fur around her ankles since they'd be tucked under the covers. And the lady answered, 'My dear, the fur keeps my *neck* warm.'"

Dom laughed, his eyes dancing.

"Yeah, my mother told me that one," Courtney said. "I didn't get how risqué it was because I was so young. I thought she was referring to nightgown creep."

"They do tend to work their way up."

Courtney pursed her lips in a pretense of priggishness. "They *do* creep up...even without assistance."

Dom laughed again and grabbed her, rolling her onto her back so that he was propped over her. His face gentled suddenly, and he smoothed her hair back from her face. "You're beautiful," he murmured. "You seem to be getting more beautiful with every day."

"You're just getting used to me."

"Then I wouldn't notice that you seem more beautiful."

She bit her lip, unsure how to reply. The joking atmosphere had vanished. Something rattled as the wind gusted and Dom looked up. He waited a moment, listening, then bent to drop a kiss on her lips. Just a light, gentle one. After the way they'd spent the afternoon, the passion seemed to have quieted at last, growing soft, like glowing embers rather than leaping flames.

He rolled a little so that he was propped on his elbow and she was free to move if she chose. Yet he was still close enough for her to reach out and touch. She liked that.

"Need anything?" he asked.

"I'm fine." She stirred a little and felt the bulge of her weapon, hidden under the edge of the tarp again. She wondered if he'd figured it out by now, and wondered why she was still concealing it.

Then she knew. It was a link to a life he didn't seem to

fully approve of. Her throat tightened a bit, and she couldn't help asking, "Do you disapprove of me?"

"Whatever gave you that idea?" He sounded astonished.

"What you said last night about justice. About what could happen to the twins if they found out their mother was murdered."

"I don't disapprove of you. I don't even disapprove of what you're doing." His eyes narrowed a bit as if he were weighing what he wanted to say. She waited, wondering if she was about to get hurt.

"I don't object to justice," he said slowly. "I don't object to those guys being brought to justice. If they were willing to do those things, they certainly shouldn't be walking free."

"Then what?"

"I told you my thinking. I don't want my kids to look at that flag and see a betrayal of the worst kind. That's a kind of innocence I don't want them to lose. At least not at this age."

She drew a deep breath. "I can honestly understand that."

"I suppose you can, after what happened to your dad."

"I remember his funeral. Every cop who could get away for hundreds of miles around was there. I remember the bagpipes. I can't hear bagpipes to this day without crying. Do Kyle and Todd remember the honors Mary received?"

"Some of them, I'm sure. I had a videographer record it for them, but I've never played it. Maybe someday they will."

"Maybe. You're right, I don't want to take that from them. And right now, I'm not even sure I could."

"Because of your suspect?"

"Some people are golden. They're untouchable, essentially, unless you can marshal enough evidence to get past all the roadblocks. I don't think that's going to happen."

"Can you live with that?"

"I have to. And I'm leaving on Monday so you can get back to your lives. So I can get back to mine."

He hesitated. "Yes, you do. Anything else would be impractical."

So all this was just impractical. He couldn't have chosen a better word to make her feel like dung. She forced herself to agree, though, hoping there was no edge in her voice. "It is."

"Yeah." He fell silent, leaving her to wonder where his thoughts roamed.

Her heart hurt, but didn't want him to know that. She had *some* pride. "We're just having a fling." Never mind that it almost killed her to categorize it that way. Never mind that she figured she was already in well over her head. He clearly wanted only to enjoy her and be done with her.

"Yeah," he said again. But when he reached for her, she pulled away.

"And I think it's over," she said shortly. They didn't pass another unnecessary word.

Morning dawned cold and gray. Over coffee and breakfast, they talked about what to do.

"I'm satisfied with what I saw yesterday," she told him. "It was fantastic. But it's cold out there and what if it rains?" Frankly, being alone with him made her feel irritable because all that remained was pain. In the morning she'd be gone, putting this place behind her before its tendrils could wrap around her heart any tighter. And, God knew, she didn't want to give him any more than she already had.

"I've got ponchos. You never travel out here without proper gear because the farther you get into the mountains the faster the weather can change. But I agree, there's a chance we might just get cold and wet. We can do this again sometime, if you ever want to come back."

If she wanted to come back? Not likely now. Hadn't he already said this was impractical? So his invitation to return was mere courtesy. And that made her feel even grumpier.

They were taking the same path home that they had followed up the mountain, but now in the brighter morning light as the clouds began to burn off, Courtney could see more of it. She loved the countryside hereabouts, the shift that was almost sudden from the flat ranchland into high mountains. She loved the fresh, dry air that sparkled with the aroma of fir trees. Around every bend in the trail she discovered some new feast for her eyes.

She caught sight of something in the woods at the same time Marti snorted and bobbed her head. "Dom? Dom…what was that?"

He drew up and looked at her. "What?"

"I saw something in the woods. Maybe a wolf?"

"What did it look like?"

"It was hard to see. Mostly gray with some white."

"Maybe it was a wolf." He eyed Marti. "She looks nervous. She must have caught a whiff of something. Come on, let's go a little faster to settle her down."

He picked up his speed and Marti followed instinctively. Courtney discovered with pleasure that she was keeping her seat more naturally and comfortably than a week ago. This was kind of neat.

At that instant something happened. At first she couldn't tell what, but Dom suddenly fell back so that he was a little behind her.

"Arnett's spooked," she heard him mutter. Immediately she thought of the wolf.

But suddenly his mount reared, screaming, Marti pivoted sideways, and she watched in horror as Dom was almost thrown. Then in almost no time at all, the horse began to stumble. Dom was out of his saddle and on the ground in an eyeblink.

That's when she heard the report echo around her. At once she slipped from her own saddle, hitting the ground, hanging on to her rein and she hurried over to Dom.

"Get down," she said to him, pushing at him.

He crouched immediately and hurried to his horse, which had fallen on its side, screaming and writhing.

"Dom."

"You get down," he snapped. "Now!"

She was already doing so, crouching so low that boulders and bushes should conceal her from almost any direction. Marti yanked on the lead rein, her eyes rolling, and she bucked once before coming to a standstill, shivering.

God, Courtney thought, the horse was exposed. But how did you get a horse to lie down?

She turned to see what Dom was doing and gasped in horror. He had his shotgun in his hands and was standing over his horse.

"Dom, get down."

"Shut up," he growled. "Some things are too important to put off." With a twisted face, he put the barrel of his gun to the horse's head and fired. Arnett fell still.

"Get over here but keep down," Dom ordered. His voice cracked. She was already on her way, fighting Marti who didn't want to get any closer to Arnett. At last she lay on the ground beside Dom.

He crouched beside her, and he didn't say a word when she felt under her sweatshirt and pulled out her service weapon.

"That," he said grimly, "was no hunter."

No, she thought. They'd been talking. They couldn't possibly have looked like deer, or antelope or anything else you might hunt around here.

Dom pointed to Arnett's flank. There was no mistaking

the bullet's entry wound. Then he pointed upslope toward the trees. "It came from there."

She started drawing lines in her head, and felt a chill race down her back. "It was supposed to hit *me*. If Arnett hadn't spooked..."

"That's my guess."

She tightened her grip on her Glock 17 and scanned the area. "We're not going to see him. Judging by the delay between Arnett's reaction and the sound of the gunshot, he's shooting from quite a distance."

"Yes. But he's got to know he missed."

"God, Dom, you shouldn't have stood up like that. He might have taken you out!"

"I couldn't let Arnett suffer." His tone was flat, concealing what she was sure was a world of anger and pain. She'd seen him with Arnett enough to know he held that horse in special affection. "There are some things you need to understand, and that's one of them."

She bridled a bit, but not much. Her attention was focused elsewhere, on the shooter and what they needed to do now. All her training argued against her heart, and she had to let training win, no matter what Dom said, no matter that he made her feel stupid in some way.

"Marti," she said. "What about Marti?"

"I don't think he's going to shoot another horse. But we have to figure out what to do fast, because he's probably coming closer. How far away do you think he was?"

Courtney had shifted into action mode, and all her recent training took over, shoving fear and everything else into the background. "I didn't time it. Far enough for us to make a break as long as he doesn't shoot again immediately. We've got to make it into the trees."

"Yeah." They both scanned the area around. Courtney pointed at what she thought was the shortest route.

"Maybe," Dom replied. "Keep your eyes peeled. I need to reload."

She kept watch over the side of the dead horse, her pistol at ready. Marti shifted impatiently, blocking her view, but at the same time she blocked the view of whoever hunted them.

"I know these guys, Dom," she said rapidly, wanting to fill him in. It was instinct: tell your partner everything. "They can move through the woods like wraiths. I'm just surprised he missed me. But he's not going to quit until he finishes the job. Not now."

For a moment, angry eyes met hers. "You were so sure nobody could find you." He bent back to slip shells into his shotgun.

She had to batter down another urge to fight with him. Adrenaline, she told herself. It was just adrenaline. Be rational. "I was," she said. "And even so, damn it, I was sure nobody would come after me when there was a witness."

"Apparently you were wrong."

She refused to answer. What was happening right now didn't make a whole lot of sense, they were both angry because they were filled with adrenaline, *so let it go.* Especially since Dom had plenty of reason to be upset about Arnett.

Dom spoke as he snapped his shotgun closed. "So okay. He's coming and we've got to take care of him. Our best advantage is that I know these mountains like the back of my hand. He won't. He can't possibly."

"No. But he'll be good anyway."

"Not as good as knowing where everything is, not as good as navigating the thick growth like it's your own backyard. Because it *is* my backyard. No navigation equipment he might have will give him an edge over me."

"Maybe not. But these guys are trained to handle all kinds of terrain. It won't slow him much."

"But it might slow him enough." Dom sounded grim. Then he rolled over onto his stomach, looking around.

She spoke. "He's going to hunt us all the way down."

"Then we need to set a trap. And one thing for sure, help will be on its way soon."

"How can you know that?"

"Because if I'm late picking up my kids, Mary's folks will call out the posse. I'm never late. But I'm going to send a message anyway."

"How so? We don't have a radio."

He smiled darkly. "We have a horse."

He took the lead rein from Courtney's hand and coaxed a terrified Marti closer. "You're going to be all the message I need, Marti."

"What do you mean?"

"I'm going to send her home. When she arrives, Ted will know something's wrong. And he knows exactly where we came and by what route."

Courtney protested as Dom rose to his knees, but he ignored her. "Dom, we need her. We can move faster."

He ignored her and unhooked the reins from Marti so she wouldn't get tangled on anything, then wrapped them in a loop around his shoulder. He held her by her bridle.

"Okay, she's going to cover us as we go to the trees."

"Dom…"

He looked at her, his eyes as flat as slate. "I don't want anything to happen to her, either. But even less do I want anything to happen to you. So this is how we play it. Whoever that shooter is, he could take us both out while we try to mount Marti. This is it."

Finally, she nodded, hating the good sense of his argument but recognizing he was right.

"Hold her bridle for minute."

Courtney stretched up an arm and slipped her fingers through it. "Poor girl," she murmured. "Poor Marti."

Dom, lying on his side, opened a saddlebag and pulled out some more shells, stuffing them in his jacket pockets. Then he took the rope he had looped on his saddle and added that to the reins on his shoulder. "Okay. We're ready. When I say go, we get up and head for those trees fast. Keep the barrel of Marti's body between you and the upslope. Understand?"

"Yes."

She understood perfectly. What he was asking of her was part of her training. She just didn't like having to use Marti as a shield, but she couldn't afford to think about that too much. Not now. Not when Dom was every bit as much risk as she.

Her mind had begun to work at top speed, the way it did when she was on a mission. One after another she weighed possible actions the shooter might take, considered the things he would be concerned about. Shoved her feelings far into the background.

"Now," said Dom.

As one they stood, keeping Marti between them and the shooter somewhere above them. Ducking beside the horse, all of them moving fast, Courtney felt as if she were running on automatic, as if she'd prepared for exactly this moment. And maybe that's what she'd been doing in Georgia.

Then they were in the woods, in a thick stand of pines. Unfortunately there was little ground cover, but there were a lot of shadows.

Dom reached into Marti's saddlebags and came out with a small wirebound notebook and pen. He scrawled across the page, then tucked it back in the saddlebag with its cover hanging out.

"What's that?" she asked.

"A note for Ted. Whoever comes after us better come armed."

Then he swatted Marti hard on her rump and said, "Home!"

The mare took off as if the minions of hell were on her heels.

"You're sure she'll go?"

"As sure as I am that Arnett's gone. And she'll go fast."

Then he looked at her. "I know the area, but you know what we're up against."

"Let's keep moving," she said. "Keep to the trees. At this point I don't care if we leave a trail."

They started at a quick walk down hill. They did not follow a straight line.

"How long do you figure it'll take help to get to us?" she asked.

"Too long. A few hours at the very best."

"Okay." She drew a breath, clearing her head. "I'm sure he's trained. If Arnett hadn't suddenly spooked, we wouldn't be talking right now."

"I get that."

"So he's going to be relentless. And he's going to not want to leave a trail. If he'd hit me with his first shot, it could have been passed off as a hunter and nobody would ever have been able to prove otherwise. Now things have changed. He's going to have to take us both out."

"Too bad he doesn't know our sheriff. Gage will never rest."

"Gage won't be able to find him. This guy won't leave anything behind to identify him, and he'll be gone from here as soon as he finishes his job."

"You're not making me feel better."

"I want to assess this clearly. I want us both to know exactly what to expect."

He nodded grimly. "Go on."

"He's moving fast right now. If anything slows him down,

it's going to be removing the bullet from your horse. He won't want to leave that behind, and since he's not sure how long he'll have after he gets to us, it's unlikely he'll leave that for later."

"Okay, so a few minutes lead time."

"At least, but probably more. Wherever he took that shot from, I'm going to guess it had to be at least a thousand yards."

"That means he had to be up really high to get a bead on us. So we have some time."

"Some, but we're going to lose a lot of it misleading him. I hope you're well-conditioned."

"What do you think?"

Despite the intensity of her focus and her emotions right now, she had to smile. "Good enough."

She picked up speed to a trot and heard him moving right alongside her. "We'll go a little farther down, then I want to set some false trails. And I want you to think of a good place to set up an ambush, a place where we'll be able to see him coming while keeping ourselves concealed."

"I know the perfect place. Down farther there's a deep ravine. If we make him cross it, we'll see him in plenty of time."

"Sounds good."

Twenty minutes later she slowed. "Okay. This is a good place. Let's trample some brush, but not too much." She pointed into the woods into a slightly open brushy area that spread between the lines of trees almost like a path. "Where does that go?"

"To a stream."

"Would it look reasonable for us to go this way?"

"If he's got a map, it sure would."

"Then let's go. Fast."

They headed at a diagonal to their original path. She didn't try to avoid breaking twigs or stirring up the pine needles. Five minutes later they reached a stream.

"Backtrack," she said. "Just try not to disturb anything this time. It matters which way the grass bends and the twigs break."

"I *do* know that much."

That meant moving slower, but she was fairly sure they had the time. Just before they reached their original path again, she saw an opening that was completely carpeted with pine needles. No flowers or grasses to break. Better yet, it had been totally unnoticeable as they had headed out on their diversion. That meant their pursuer wouldn't see it, either, until he was backtracking, too.

She stopped. "Pick your feet up. Don't scuff."

It was an unnatural way to walk but when they reached the other side of the opening, she looked back and could see almost nothing to mark their passing.

"Good. He won't see we came this way until he's backtracking from the stream, and the stream should delay him for a while as he looks for a point where we might have crossed it. When he comes back, he'll see this clearing. Our bootprints are faint, but we'll have gained some time so it won't matter if he sees them." Then she led the way back to the edge of the woods near the trail they'd followed originally.

"I thought we wanted him to follow us."

"We do. But we want time to set up an ambush. We'll do that a few more times. Before we get to the place you want to set up the ambush, I want to make a wide circle leading toward the ravine."

She barely glanced at him. Adrenaline had a life expectancy and hers was fading a bit. It would come back in a rush later, but meanwhile she couldn't bear the look she was sure was on his face.

"Dom."

"Yeah." His voice sounded as tight as a spring.

"You know I wouldn't have stayed if I had honestly believed this could happen."

He didn't answer as they climbed over a rock and hit the ground on the other side. "I know," he said finally. "I know. And neither of us has been thinking too clearly."

Everything inside her winced. No, they hadn't been thinking clearly. That was obvious now. She'd been drawn into a life she didn't have a right to, had allowed herself to grow feelings that she wasn't entitled to, and all the while he'd just been having a fling. It was almost enough to make her wish she were dead already.

Well over an hour later, having left another false trail and the wide circle she wanted to make, they reached the ravine. As Dom had promised, on the far side she saw possibilities for an ambush.

Dom was able to guide her to a place where they could clamber down with relative ease, making a minimal disturbance. On the other side, with wet, muddy boots, they had little hope of concealing their passage entirely.

Nor did Courtney any longer want to. Now she wanted the shooter to be sure he was on their trail. They climbed up into the forest again and before long she'd picked a good spot.

"I want two angles of fire," she said. "He can't go for us both at once if we separate, and cross fire will give us an edge."

She glanced at Dom and read respect in his face. "You're good," he said.

"He probably knows exactly what I do, so don't pat my back yet. First let's make it look like we kept on going."

That was easy enough. They ran, deliberately leaving muddy footprints, through a not-quite dry area where water must have pooled recently. Easy to make it look like they were still racing downhill.

But afterward she changed tack. "Time for stocking feet."

"What?"

"No trail. Right now our boots are dropping mud everywhere."

So off they came, and the two of them crept back to their vantage point. Just before Courtney left him in the position she'd chosen for him, Dom grabbed her, hugged her and kissed her hard.

She wanted to dissolve, she wanted to just melt into him and forget everything else. Quickly she pushed him away, certain that he was acting on feelings that had nothing to do with permanence. Nothing at all. He'd said so. And she couldn't afford to be distracted by anything right now, not him, not her feelings.

"Stay flat," she said almost tonelessly, "and move as little as possible to reduce your heat signature. If you see him, don't move a muscle. He won't cross the ravine until he scans with binoculars because he knows he'll be in the open."

"Okay."

She touched his arm lightly, unable to stop herself. "Be careful. Please be careful."

Then she slipped away to her own hiding place, feeling as if she had just cracked open her heart and let her fears spill onto the ground. Fears she wasn't familiar with, fears she had never allowed herself to feel before. Fears she had refused to ever experience again after the death of her father.

For the first time she realized why men quickly learned to avoid her. She wasn't just bossy. She'd turned into an ice queen who held them at bay.

Looking back suddenly, propelled by the fact that she could be dead before this day was out, she saw a woman who had lived in a self-made bubble, serving intellect and only one emotion: her need for justice. Mary had been the first person to get past that in any meaningful way.

And look where it had gotten her: more pain. Enough pain and anger that she was still hunting Mary's killers. Just as she would have hunted her dad's if she'd been old enough. But the real sorrow in it all was that she'd brought danger to Dom, and through him to his boys.

Oh, she had become a lovely person. Bitterness filled her as she looked at herself with utter clarity.

Maybe, she thought, if she survived this, she should give some thought to learning to let go.

It certainly might do her a world of good.

Chapter 13

A torrent of emotions ripped through Dom as he crawled into his hiding place, shielded by a rock from view across the river, lying on grass that was still damp, ignoring a nest of burrs.

So Courtney was leaving in the morning. The deadline had finally arrived. Part of him felt furious that she'd blown into his life this way and was ready to blow out again just as quickly. A fling, she'd called it.

Yeah, except he resented the hell out of that. He didn't like feeling used. Never had. And equally bad to his way of thinking was the way she'd brought a killer to his door.

Oh, she said she had been positive nobody had followed her, and maybe she had believed it herself. But here they were, one of his best horses dead, and hiding now for their lives. What if the boys had been with them?

He couldn't even bear that thought.

But when he tested inside himself, poking around as if hunting a sore tooth, what he found was a man who wasn't angry at Courtney at all, except for her decision to leave, and the way she had pushed him away last night, as if done with him. Apparently she was.

What kind of fool was he anyway? Mary had loved him, but even she hadn't been happy with the ranch alone. What in the world had made him get involved with another woman who would always want and need to be somewhere else?

Idiot!

An hour passed, maybe more. The clouds had burned away and the sun rose higher, heating the ground which would make them harder to see if their hunter had thermal gear. Courtney had hardly dared hope for that.

The longer they held still, the more the forest wildlife resumed its life. Squirrels chattered. Bigger things moved around beneath the trees and in the bushes. The wind picked up, making treetops whisper and creak like aging bones.

She thought of the wolf she might have seen, and wondered if she was lying in some pack's territory, being observed right now. The thought didn't frighten her.

Her emotions had reached stasis, utter calm. Months of training had given her that ability, to grow quiet inside and just wait. She doubted Dom had the same cold comfort.

Then she saw their hunter. Just a flicker among the shadows beneath the trees across the ravine. Woodland camouflage covered him head to toe, and he'd even painted his face. But Courtney had long since learned to see past patterns to shapes. It was essential for survival in her new unit.

That shape was not natural.

It paused, still just inside the woods, and she thought he lifted his arms. Binoculars.

She looked toward Dom and saw that he was looking her way. He jerked his head, indicating he had seen it, too.

Time dragged on leaden feet. Finally, whatever he'd seen,

it hadn't worried him. He emerged from the shadows and clambered down the far side of the ravine.

The sound of rushing water washed out the sounds of the hunter's approach. The next time she knew where he was, his head was emerging over the edge of the ravine.

He clambered up, crouched, looked around. And as clearly as if he had announced it out loud, she saw him catch sight of their now drying, muddy boot prints.

He straightened, obviously sure he had a longer trek ahead of him.

Come on, she thought impatiently. *Just come on.*

He eased toward them, scanning the woods but more intent on the footprints he was following. Not so bright, Courtney thought. Not bright at all. Obviously whoever had sent him hadn't been able to send the best. Or had sent someone who hadn't done this kind of thing for a while. A missed shot, and now a glaring lack of caution.

She tightened her grip on her pistol getting ready.

Then Dom horrified her by rising from the brush and aiming his shotgun at the guy.

"Stop and drop it," Dom ordered.

Of course the guy didn't obey. Instead he started to swing his rifle toward Dom. Courtney didn't hesitate. Without moving from her hide, she pulled the trigger on her Glock.

And missed. The guy had moved just as she squeezed her trigger, just enough that she'd missed. And now he knew where they both were. She started to fire again, but the guy took a shot her way first, causing her to duck.

Dom burst out of the bushes and ran right at their attacker. Courtney was horrified, but galvanized instantly, she rose.

Dom's race toward the man drew his attention. He fired quickly at Dom, missing, and then Courtney added her own shot to the fray.

Missing again. Damn it, she knew how to shoot better than this.

But even as she cussed herself, her shot had bought time. Dom launched himself through the air like a football player making a tackle and caught the guy right around the knees, bringing them both to the ground.

But the hunter was still armed. Too well trained to let go of his gun, and now Courtney couldn't even shoot for fear of hitting Dom.

She jumped out of her hide and ran toward them, but they were rolling on the ground now as Dom fought to disarm the guy. If she hadn't been so pumped on adrenaline, her heart would have stopped. At any instant the guy's rifle could go off and hit Dom.

But when she reached them, she saw that Dom was aware of that. His arms strained to keep the rifle pointed away while the guy punched at him with his other hand.

Making a quick decision, she darted around them and put her foot on the rifle barrel, keeping it pointed away. Then she leveled her pistol and said, "Stop or I'll shoot."

She felt the rifle barrel jerk under foot and leaned on it even more heavily. The two men were still so wound together, still struggling, and she really didn't dare pull the trigger.

And neither of them listened to her anyway. Dom got a good solid punch to the guy's jaw. Then he got punched in his side, letting out an "oof."

They started to roll again, a tangle of limbs, but that time the rifle didn't move with the bad guy. As they rolled away, she took the opportunity to snatch it up and sling it over her shoulder, safely out of the way. The guy undoubtedly had other weapons, though....

And just as she had the thought, she saw it. A knife. He'd released the rifle to pull the blade from its sheath, and damn, it was heading straight for Dom.

Without further thought, left with no choice, she fired. The knife flew away along with a piece of the guy's hand.

He howled. As pain ricocheted through his body, his first instinct was to fight harder, but Dom had him now in the vise grip of his thighs, in powerful hands on his shoulder. A grip he'd managed to get while the other guy opened up to try to come at him with the knife.

"Damn it," Courtney yelled, "I'm gonna shoot you, you bastard."

Somehow that seemed to get through. The guy's eyes tracked to her and saw her standing over them, pistol in a practiced, two-handed grip. And maybe he saw something in her eyes, because, so help her, if he laid into Dom again she was going to remove him from the human race.

"Don't move. Don't even twitch."

He was cussing, as well he might. Blood ran from his damaged hand like water. He started to move and she stepped in, putting her foot on his neck. "Don't even twitch," she said, repeating the warning. Without glancing away she told Dom, "Search him. He's got other weapons. And watch his feet."

Dom had a simple solution for that. He pivoted, keeping the guy's hips between his thighs, and pulled Marti's reins off his shoulder. Then, experienced roper that he was, he used them to bind the guy's ankles tightly together.

Then, with absolutely no compunction at all, after yanking the guy's pack off his shoulders, he pulled out the other man's rope and used it to bind the guy's wrists just as tightly, hog-tying them to his ankles.

"Now search him," Courtney insisted.

"I'm bleeding, damn it," the guy squawked.

"I care?" Dom said tautly. "You killed my horse, you SOB. You tried to kill my girl."

His girl? But Courtney couldn't allow herself to get distracted now. Once she was sure Dom had removed every potential weapon from the guy, making a small pile of knives, a pistol, a garrote and some other handy little, easily concealable items that could be used in a fight, she relaxed a bit.

"Let's tie him to a tree," she said. "Then I'll look at his wound."

They trussed him sitting up against a tree, his arms constrained by the rope around the tree. Only then did she pay attention to his hand. In his pack she found some powdered antibiotic and a T-shirt. Quickly and efficiently she bandaged what was left, not caring if she hurt him.

Another search of his pack revealed little except survival gear. This man had come on a covert operation. Nothing to identify him at all.

She swore. Then she looked at Dom who was sitting on the ground with one knee up, his arm resting on it.

"That was a damn fool thing you did," she told him.

"You think I was going to let him get a shot at you?"

"The way I had it set up…" She trailed off. Then, "You should have done it my way. You could have been killed."

"You care?"

That felt like a gut punch, despite the fact she was in hyperdrive after a close call, still trying to operate as a professional, still trying to keep her head clear. "Yes!" she snapped. "I do care. A whole helluva lot."

Then she sat back on her heels, told him their captive he was under arrest and recited his rights. When he acknowledged he understood them, her voice hardened.

"Talk," she said.

"I got nothing to say."

"You got plenty to say," she said harshly. "Did Metcalfe put you up to this?"

She caught his expression as she said the name, and she

knew, absolutely knew. And the fact that she knew the name seemed to take the wind out of the guy's sails.

"You know?" he asked hoarsely.

"I know. So unless you want six consecutive life terms along with him, you might want to start talking. I'm still with NCIS. I can still get you a deal."

"We could always just shoot him here," Dom said. "My friend the sheriff would consider it justified as self-defense. And frankly, so would I."

Courtney glanced at him, astonished to hear such a thing come out of Dom's mouth. It seemed so unlike him. But there was no mistaking the fury on his face. *His horse and his girl.* Maybe this guy had an unexpected side to him. Maybe the Wild West hadn't completely died out.

And that's when the story spilled.

Metcalfe had been the ringleader, start to finish. He'd started worrying almost from the moment Mary met Courtney for the first time, because Mary was working with some of his victims. People who could identify him if they ever surmounted the wall of social shame and fear that kept them quiet.

This guy didn't know the details of how Metcalfe had arranged for the convoy to be reduced to only one Humvee, or even how he had staged her shooting, but he knew Metcalfe had been behind it all. Metcalfe had told him so when he explained why Courtney had to be eliminated.

"Why did you agree to come after me?" Courtney asked.

"Because Metcalfe said he'd pin the whole thing on me. All of it. And if anybody could pull those strings, it's Metcalfe, damn it. He'd have made the other guys say it was all me. All of it, and they'd claim I shot my mouth off and that was how they found out." He closed his eyes a minute. "You don't know what that guy gets away with. You don't have a clue. He can still get you."

Courtney finally asked him point-blank, "Were you involved in any of it?"

The guy sighed and let his head fall back against the tree. "Yeah," he said finally. "Yeah. I was a lookout."

The next couple of hours passed slowly. Courtney gave the guy, who finally identified himself as Barry Hardwicke, plenty of water from his own stash. His blood loss seemed to have stopped and when he asked for food, Dom fed him a granola bar out of his rucksack.

Courtney finally sat back against a tree herself, and Dom joined her.

"Are you okay?" he asked her.

"Oh, I'm fine. I got my answers. I'm just sorry as hell that I cost you Arnett."

"You didn't cost me Arnett. *He* did. Just like you didn't cost me Mary. Crap, Courtney, next thing you'll be telling me is that you were somehow responsible for what happened to your father."

She tilted her head to look at him, realizing that now that the adrenaline had worn off, she was as exhausted as she could ever remember feeling. "Do I seem that off-kilter?" She hated to ask, but if that's how he saw her, she needed to know now.

"No." He shook his head. "I was just trying to tell you to cut it out. You didn't do anything to deserve a killer on your tail. No more than Mary did. God, this is ugly."

"Yeah. Start to finish. It could hardly get uglier."

"Do you think you'll get this Metcalfe guy now?"

"Probably. If Barry here knows who else was involved, I can guarantee folks are going to start singing in order to cut deals."

"So it's good."

"For me. But..." She bit her lip. "Your boys."

"I just won't tell them. They don't need to know any of

this. Not one bit. And I'm sure when Gage gets here with his posse, he'll understand that, too."

"Okay. Okay." She sighed and closed her eyes for a minute. "I couldn't stand hurting those boys."

He slipped his arm around her shoulders and held her close to his side.

"I hope," he said, "that the posse arrives soon. That guy isn't looking too good."

"No." But at the moment it was hard to care. Gathering her energy, afraid that if she let herself relax too long, afraid of what Dom's arm around her made her feel, she went over to check Barry out. "The bleeding has almost stopped." Feeling his cheeks and forehead, she noted that they were dry. "I don't think he's in shock."

She sat cross-legged on the ground beside him. "Why don't you give me some names?" she asked.

So he did, and she wrote them all down on a piece of paper she found in his rucksack along with a pen. Then she gave him some more water. He drank thirstily.

"Help will be here soon," she assured him. But for an instant it was hard to feel even that basic human compassion. This man had tried to kill her. He was part of a group that had killed Mary and raped women and girls. He could have killed Dom.

It was hard, just then, to care if he lived or died. Except that she needed him, so somehow he had to live.

She loathed the ugliness in herself, but there it was.

She was almost as bad as he was. But just almost. Because she made sure he got plenty of water and she'd patched his wound. She had absolutely no doubt that he wouldn't have shown her or Dom the same mercy.

But there were a couple of other questions she wanted answers to. "Was it you who shot at me last week? And why were you stupid enough to come after me when you knew you'd have to take out someone else, as well?"

"Metcalfe," he said, and groaned. "Metcalfe. Something set him off this past week. He insisted it was now or never."

The photo, she realized. Metcalfe must indeed have his file flagged somehow, and had been alerted that someone had done a face match on him. Oh, man, she almost shuddered. This was going to get ugly and reach into places that... She halted herself midstream. No, they wouldn't let that happen. The higher-ups would prevent it. But she was certain now that she'd get to make her case against Metcalfe. The rest of the bastards who'd protected the guy could slink away under their rocks again.

The important thing was to get the murderer and rapists. And she had enough now to do that.

Hanging on to every shred of strength, she forced herself to remain icy, even though she wanted nothing now but to start shaking in reaction, to rage at what these men had done to Mary, to those Iraqi women, to Dom and his sons. What they had tried to do to her didn't even seem to enter into it really.

Besides, watching the prisoner was a good excuse not to look at Dom, not to look at all she could never have. All of it belonged to another woman.

The shaft of ice that pierced her heart right then felt as if it would kill her.

They heard rescue arriving long before it appeared. The drum of hoofbeats grew from more than just a sense of something more felt than heard until there seemed to be a thunder rolling up the mountain.

Courtney gaped when at last rescuers began to appear on both sides of the ravine. Not only were there mounted sheriff's deputies, but there appeared to be a phalanx of local ranchers and cowboys, all armed, all of them wearing determined faces.

"Told you there'd be a posse," Dom said.

He stood up and shouted to get their attention as they approached. Those who could, including Gage Dalton and Micah Parish, wheeled toward them. The others on the far side of the ravine, halted, too, and began to look for ways to cross.

It was over. At least this part was. Courtney sagged back against the tree and let Dom explain everything. She'd have a job to do later, but right now all she wanted to do was bask in a strange sense of lightness, as if a burden had been shed for good.

The next arrival was a helicopter, which hovered above the trees and lowered a basket into the small clearing. Ropes were exchanged for handcuffs as they loaded Barry into a basket stretcher, and the cuffs were attached to the stretcher itself. One of deputies wound his finger around, telling the chopper to raise the patient. A few minutes later, the roar of the blades disappeared back down the mountain.

Little by little, the milling men and women began to disperse back down the mountain, calling cheerfully back and forth now that everything was okay.

Then Ted arrived, leading two saddled horses. "Figured you two might need a lift," he said.

"Much appreciated," Dom told him. "Arnett's back up the mountain a ways. I need to get my saddle and gear."

"I'll do that," Ted said. "You and your lady just head on home. One of these folks'll help me."

"Thanks, Ted."

Ted shrugged. "I called Mary's parents. They know you got held up. I didn't tell them why. Didn't want to upset them."

"Thanks again."

"Seems the least I could do." Ted touched the brim of his hat, made a gesture to another man and they set off.

Dom passed the reins of one of the mares to Courtney. "She's not quite as placid as Marti, but she's good. Think you're ready?"

"You know what? I do believe I am."

Approaching the mare, she patted her neck and let her sniff her hand. "What's your name, beautiful?"

"That's Cindy Lou."

Courtney shot a look at Dom. "Tell me you're joking."

"Blame it on Kyle. Of course," he added, looking at his own mount, "this guy is Grinch. For good reason."

Courtney slipped her foot in the stirrup and swung up into the saddle. Immediately she felt the strength of a younger, more active horse beneath her, and she thrilled to the sensation of power. Dom adjusted the stirrups a bit for her, then swung up on the gelding who immediately sidled a bit as if unsure he liked this.

"I thought your horses never misbehave," Courtney said.

"There's an exception to every rule." Dom winked. "Actually, he's a pretty good cutting horse. But I don't think either of them are all too fond of the smell of blood. Let's get out of here."

It was amazing, after the horrible hours they'd just been through, that the day felt so beautiful, and her mood so light.

She was probably just high on survival, she thought. High because the nightmare was behind her. The bad guys would go down, they'd survived a killer and caught him and...

And she was with Dom. Probably for the last time.

Tomorrow, or whenever they let her prisoner out of the hospital, she'd be on her way back to her old life, to deal with a case that was probably going to bite her just as hard as she'd bitten it, given who was involved.

But she wouldn't be staying here. She hadn't been asked to stay. And even if she had, she still had duties that had to be completed before she could even think of such a thing.

Her mood dived a bit at the thought. Clearly she had some serious thinking to do.

Because all of sudden, she didn't at all want to go back to her old life. No. Whatever did or did not happen with Dom, she knew with absolute certainty as she rode down a mountainside in Wyoming, that she did not want to go back to the life and the person she had been.

The kids were in bed, unaware that bad things had happened that day. Dom had tucked them in just as if it were any other night, telling them not one thing about the day's events.

On the threshold of their room, he turned off the light and stood still for a few minutes. Courtney was downstairs, and he felt as if he was facing doom. She'd made it clear she was going, she'd even pushed him away last night after calling their lovemaking a fling.

Of course she was going. She'd always been going. The question was why he'd let himself get so involved that the inevitable was going to hurt. It wasn't as if she'd misled him in any way.

Yet now there was going to be another hole in his life, another hole at the ranch. He wanted to kick his own butt for being stupid enough to make the same kind of choice twice. Or maybe even a worse one, because Mary had wanted to live out here, she'd never wanted to go some other place. She just had other things to do.

Courtney, on the other hand, was a visitor and had never intended to be anything more.

On feet that felt as heavy as solid lead, he went downstairs. Time to be a man and say goodbye.

He entered the living room and she watched him from those

smoky blue eyes. She didn't look a whole lot better than he felt, but there was nothing he could do about that. She'd had a rough day, and she was leaving. His options were gone.

"After I got the news about Mary," he said quietly, "I took the boys to their grandparents. Then I got me a horse, a few supplies, and I rode hard until the horse had to stop. And then I rode some more. I rode like I could get away from it."

The corners of her mouth trembled and her eyes saddened. "I'm so, so sorry."

"I don't want you to be sorry. But I'm feeling like getting on a horse again and riding until we both drop."

He watched expressions play over her face, so fast he couldn't read them.

"I don't… Dom, what are you trying to say? I'm not Mary. I can't be Mary."

"I know you're not Mary. I'm not asking you to be Mary. I know you're Courtney, and Courtney's leaving for good."

She caught her breath. "And that makes you want to ride until you drop?"

"Yeah." There, he'd said it.

"Oh, God." She sighed. A tear trembled on her lash.

"Look, I just need to know one thing for myself before you go."

"Yes?"

"Did you mean it when you said you cared about me, or was this all just a fling? Was I just a handy stud?

She drew a sharp breath, and something flared in her eyes. She spoke sharply. "Of course I meant it. I said I care a helluva lot, and I do. But you don't want me."

"Who the hell said I don't want you?"

"You can't possibly. I'm just your worst nightmare, a career woman who is going away."

"That was never my worst nightmare. My worst nightmare is losing the woman I love."

She had opened her mouth, as if to launch into a tirade, but the instant his words penetrated, her entire expression changed. He watched, hardly daring to trust his own senses, as hope dawned on her face.

"You mean that?" she asked finally in a thin voice.

"I wouldn't have said it otherwise. I know you've got a life elsewhere. I know you're going to have to go away. Well, I handled that before, I can handle it again." His fists clenched. "The only thing I need to know is if you'll come back."

Her face twisted with pain, and he thought, *This is it. She's going to tell me she'll never come back, that she doesn't want a rancher with two sons, all the work, all the boring lifestyle. Why the hell would she, anyway?*

But then she stood, and walked over to him, until they stood just inches apart. And her words hit him like cool, refreshing springwater.

"I don't want to leave. I don't want to go back to my job."

"But…"

She put a finger over his lips. "Shh," she said softly. "I've been thinking about this constantly. I love it here. I don't want to go back to my old life, with you or without you. But I thought…I thought you didn't want me. How could you?"

He didn't even want to sort through that mountain of misunderstanding. He did the only thing he could. He pulled her close and kissed her until both of them were gasping for air. "That's how. And that's just the start."

He looked at her bruised lips, saw them begin to smile. Her first smile that day. Like a bird desperately trying to take flight, his heart began to lift. "You really mean it? You want to stay?"

"I was never more serious in my life. But I'll have to go back at least temporarily to take care of this guy. Once he finishes singing, they'll probably pass the case to someone else."

"And if they don't?"

She shrugged. "I have my answers. I guess that's enough."

"Wow."

She smiled. "That means?"

"That's a huge thing for you."

"Well, I figured a few things out. And you're right about at least some of it. I think I've replaced everything in my life with a quest for justice because my dad's killer was never found. But I don't seem to feel the need to do that anymore. At least not in the same way."

"So you'd take on a widower, twin boys and a ranch?"

"Nothing could make me happier."

"What if you get bored? Every day is pretty much the same around here."

"Every day in my job is usually pretty much the same. It's like that thing pilots say, 'hours of sheer boredom punctuated by seconds of sheer terror.' Most of it is humdrum. Truthfully. Just routine. And if I'm no longer thirsting for justice, then it's going to become even more routine."

"Just so long as you understand. If you need to keep the job, I'm not opposed. If you get bored and want to find a job around here, maybe with the sheriff or the state, I'm not opposed."

She reached up, cupping his face in her hands. "I want to stay. Other questions are for another day."

"The boys are falling in love with you, too," he said quietly.

"I can't tell you how I felt when they wanted to hug me. I want to hug them every night, Dom."

"I'd like that, too. So...Courtney?"

"Yes?" Her breath was coming faster as their hips made contact and he hardened against her.

"Will you marry me? In a few months? Whenever you're ready?"

"Yes," she said, feeling her heart lift and every cell in her body begin to sing. "Oh, yes, Dom, I want that a whole lot."

"Good." He lifted her and her legs immediately wrapped around his hips, even though he had a good grip on her. "Do you mind sharing my bed?"

"I love you," she murmured.

"I love you, too. Always."

He paused at the top of the stairs until she looked up at him again. "Just tell me you're sure."

"I'm sure. All I want now is you. I finished my final mission."

And so had Mary, he thought as he carried her into his bedroom.

There was no doubt in his mind.

* * * * *

Don't miss the next book in Rachel Lee's miniseries
CONARD COUNTY: THE NEXT GENERATION—
JUST A COWBOY,
available soon from Harlequin Romantic Suspense.

Harlequin®

ROMANTIC
SUSPENSE

COMING NEXT MONTH

Available May 31, 2011

You can find more information on upcoming
Harlequin® titles, free excerpts and more at
www.HarlequinInsideRomance.com.

REQUEST YOUR FREE BOOKS!
2 FREE NOVELS PLUS 2 FREE GIFTS!

◆ Harlequin®

ROMANTIC
SUSPENSE

Sparked by Danger, Fueled by Passion.

YES! Please send me 2 FREE Harlequin® Romantic Suspense novels and my 2 FREE gifts (gifts are worth about $10). After receiving them, if I don't wish to receive any more books, I can return the shipping statement marked "cancel." If I don't cancel, I will receive 4 brand-new novels every month and be billed just $4.24 per book in the U.S. or $4.99 per book in Canada. That's a saving of at least 15% off the cover price! It's quite a bargain! Shipping and handling is just 50¢ per book in the U.S. and 75¢ per book in Canada.* I understand that accepting the 2 free books and gifts places me under no obligation to buy anything. I can always return a shipment and cancel at any time. Even if I never buy another book, the two free books and gifts are mine to keep forever.

240/340 SDN FC95

Name _____ (PLEASE PRINT) _____

Address _____ Apt. # _____

City _____ State/Prov. _____ Zip/Postal Code _____

Signature (if under 18, a parent or guardian must sign) _____

Mail to the **Reader Service:**

IN U.S.A.: P.O. Box 1867, Buffalo, NY 14240-1867
IN CANADA: P.O. Box 609, Fort Erie, Ontario L2A 5X3

Not valid for current subscribers to Harlequin Romantic Suspense books.

Want to try two free books from another line?
Call 1-800-873-8635 or visit www.ReaderService.com.

* Terms and prices subject to change without notice. Prices do not include applicable taxes. Sales tax applicable in N.Y. Canadian residents will be charged applicable taxes. Offer not valid in Quebec. This offer is limited to one order per household. All orders subject to credit approval. Credit or debit balances in a customer's account(s) may be offset by any other outstanding balance owed by or to the customer. Please allow 4 to 6 weeks for delivery. Offer available while quantities last.

Your Privacy—The Reader Service is committed to protecting your privacy. Our Privacy Policy is available online at www.ReaderService.com or upon request from the Reader Service.

We make a portion of our mailing list available to reputable third parties that offer products we believe may interest you. If you prefer that we not exchange your name with third parties, or if you wish to clarify or modify your communication preferences, please visit us at www.ReaderService.com/consumerschoice or write to us at Reader Service Preference Service, P.O. Box 9062, Buffalo, NY 14269. Include your complete name and address.

HRS11

Harlequin® Blaze™ brings you
New York Times *and* USA TODAY *bestselling author*
Vicki Lewis Thompson with three new steamy titles
from the bestselling miniseries SONS OF CHANCE

Chance isn't just the last name of these rugged
Wyoming cowboys—it's their motto, too!

Read on for a sneak peek at the first title,
SHOULD'VE BEEN A COWBOY

Available June 2011 only from Harlequin® Blaze™.

"THANKS FOR NOT TURNING ON THE LIGHTS," Tyler said. "I'm a mess."

"Not in my book." Even in low light, Alex had a good view of her yellow shirt plastered to her body. It was all he could do not to reach for her, mud and all. But the next move needed to be hers, not his.

She slicked her wet hair back and squeezed some water out of the ends as she glanced upward. "I like the sound of the rain on a tin roof."

"Me, too."

She met his gaze briefly and looked away. "Where's the sink?"

"At the far end, beyond the last stall."

Tyler's running shoes squished as she walked down the aisle between the rows of stalls. She glanced sideways at Alex. "So how much of a cowboy are you these days? Do you ride the range and stuff?"

"I ride." He liked being able to say that. "Why?"

"Just wondered. Last summer, you were still a city boy. You even told me you weren't the cowboy type, but you're…different now."

HBEXP0611

He wasn't sure if that was a good thing or a bad thing. Maybe she preferred city boys to cowboys. "How am I different?"

"Well, you dress differently, and your hair's a little longer. Your face seems a little more chiseled, but maybe that's because of your hair. Also, there's something else, something harder to define, an attitude…"

"Are you saying I have an attitude?"

"Not in a bad way. It's more like a quiet confidence."

He was flattered, but still he had to laugh. "I just admitted a while ago that I have all kinds of doubts about this event tomorrow. That doesn't seem like quiet confidence to me."

"This isn't about your job, it's about…your…" She took a deep breath. "It's about your sex appeal, okay? I have no business talking about it, because it will only make me want to do things I shouldn't do." She started toward the end of the barn. "Now, where's that sink? We need to get cleaned up and go back to the house. Dinner is probably ready, and I—"

He spun her around and pulled her into his arms, mud and all. "Let's do those things." Then he kissed her, knowing that she would kiss him back, knowing that this time he would take that kiss where he wanted it to go. And she would let him.

Follow Tyler and Alex's wild adventures in
SHOULD'VE BEEN A COWBOY
Available June 2011 only from Harlequin® Blaze™
wherever books are sold.

SPECIAL EDITION

Life, Love and Family

LOVE CAN BE FOUND IN THE MOST UNLIKELY PLACES, ESPECIALLY WHEN YOU'RE NOT LOOKING FOR IT...

Failed marriages, broken families and disappointment. Cecilia and Brandon have both been unlucky in love and life and are ripe for an intervention. Good thing Brandon's mother happens to stumble upon this matchmaking project. But will Brandon be able to open his eyes and get away from his busy career to see that all he needs is right there in front of him?

FIND OUT IN

WHAT THE SINGLE DAD WANTS...

BY *USA TODAY* BESTSELLING AUTHOR

MARIE FERRARELLA

AVAILABLE IN JUNE 2011
WHEREVER BOOKS ARE SOLD.

www.eHarlequin.com

SE0611MF